# Ⅰ Dresses of Red and Gold

Also by Robin Klein

*People Might Hear You*
*Hating Alison Ashley*
*Halfway Across the Galaxy and Turn Left*
*Games . . .*
*Laurie Loved Me Best*
*Against the Odds*
*Came Back to Show You I Could Fly*
*Tearaways*
*All in the Blue Unclouded Weather*

# Dresses of Red and Gold

## Robin Klein

Viking

Viking
Penguin Books Australia Ltd
487 Maroondah Highway, PO Box 257
Ringwood, Victoria 3134, Australia
Penguin Books Ltd
Harmondsworth, Middlesex, England
Viking Penguin, A Division of Penguin Books USA Inc.
375 Hudson Street, New York, New York 10014, USA
Penguin Books Canada Limited
10 Alcorn Avenue, Toronto, Ontario, Canada M4V 1E4
Penguin Books (N.Z.) Ltd
182-190 Wairau Road, Auckland 10, New Zealand

First published by Penguin Books Australia, 1992
10 9 8 7 6 5 4 3 2 1
Copyright © Robin Klein, 1992

Typeset in Sabon 12/14 pt by Midland Typesetters, Maryborough, Victoria
Made and printed in Australia by Australian Print Group, Maryborough, Victoria

National Library of Australia
Cataloguing-in-Publication data:

Klein, Robin, 1936-
Dresses of red and gold.

ISBN 0 670 84733 X.

I. Title.

A823.3

*Acknowledgements*
The quotation on p. 4 is from the poem 'To Autumn' by John Keats, and the quotation on p. 33 is
from 'The Destruction of Sennacherib' by Lord Byron.

# ✐ Contents

For Alison Aprhys

# ✐ Bogeyman

'What a lot of rubbish! People in uniform all look exactly alike in snapshots,' said Heather Melling, who felt obliged to squelch from time to time because of being the eldest. 'It was probably just a stray soldier from another unit wandered in.'

'He stepped on a land mine and got blown to smithereens,' Isobel repeated, unsquelched. 'But later on when all the fighting was over they took a group photo, and when they printed it – there he was! Looking over someone's shoulder in the back row and giving the victory sign – except he was a bit fuzzy around the edges . . . '

'So would you be if you'd stepped on a mine.'

'It happens to be true, because I read about it in a magazine. It was this bloke, all right, come back from the dead to be in the photo with his mates.'

'Don't talk about creepy things when we're here all by ourselves,' Vivienne pleaded, but as she was the youngest, nobody took the slightest notice.

'There's another thing I read in a magazine. It was in England, everyone woke up in the morning and found these

✐ 1

enormous footprints in the snow. They travelled in a dead straight line all across the countryside, only they didn't go around things, they went right over. Even over church roofs and steeples, mile after mile of footprints – then they just sort of petered out in the middle of nowhere. People said they were cloven.'

'Cloven – you mean like cows? Cows can't get up on church roofs.'

'Cows aren't the only ones who've got cloven hooves. Or horns, either, for that matter . . . '

Vivienne poked the fire to make it crackle and to distract herself from Isobel. It wasn't a good time to be telling weird stories with the autumn wind moaning around the old house and throwing handfuls of splintery rain against the windows. The ceiling light flickered, and she glanced at the mantelpiece to make sure the emergency candle and box of matches were in place. Mum couldn't be relied upon to supervise that; during the last power failure they'd found a banana absent-mindedly wedged into the candlestick. A loose sheet of iron on the roof clattered, and she thought of cloven hooves, but tugged her mind resolutely away to concentrate on the toast. Toast made in front of the living-room fire and spread with bacon dripping always tasted wonderful, specially with cocoa.

'Hey, I just thought – wouldn't it be spooky if you poured a mug of cocoa, then turned your back for a minute and when you turned around the mug was empty?' Isobel said.

'Not in this house it wouldn't, that sort of thing happens quite often,' Cathy said. 'I'll tell you something really spooky, though, that serial on the wireless where they kept hearing a voice croaking, "Water . . . water . . .". You should have seen Viv – she was too scared to go down the back at night while it was on. So we had to go with her – even when it turned out the voice was only a parrot trapped in an air vent . . . If you're not eating that last slice of toast, chuck it over here.'

'Toast and bacon dripping,' Isobel grumbled. 'You never have anything elegant to eat at your house. If I'd known you were only having this for supper I'd have stayed home and practised my Spanish dancing.'

'You weren't even invited in the first place, Isobel Dion – you just showed up!' Heather said indignantly. 'I'm not even sure I should be letting you, with Dad up the bush and Mum stopping the night at Aunty Cessie's and neither of them here to say if you can or not.'

'Well, you can't make me go home now, it would be like turfing someone out in a snowstorm . . . Did you ever read that whodunit where a lady gets murdered in a little garden summer-house and there's been a snow blizzard, but – and here comes the creepy part – whoever did it never left any tracks!'

'What was the stupid thing doing in a summer-house in the middle of a blizzard?' Cathy asked. 'She would have froze to death, anyhow, so the murderer just got in first. I can go one better than that – I read this story once where someone got stabbed with an icicle and the police never found the murder weapon because it melted!'

'I wish you'd all talk about something else,' Vivienne said. The wind seemed to be strengthening, probing all the chinks in the house, but the living-room was snug with its dancing fire and new window curtains. Mum had made them from an old mosquito net, sewing bobbles around the hems. Vivienne watched the rain silvering the panes behind the net, thinking how romantic autumn was. ' "Season of mists and mellow fruitfulness...",' she whispered to herself.

'Do you realise people going by can peer in through those net curtains?' Isobel said. 'I know you don't get much traffic this far up Sawmill Road, but there's always the chance of awful old swaggies looking for a free meal. Or escaped lunatics...though I guess that wouldn't trouble you all that much. You're used to your dad, so they'd just seem normal if they came knocking on the door.'

'Knocking thrice,' Cathy said. 'That's what they always say in books – knock thrice and enter. I used to think thrice was a person when I was little, "He knocked, Thrice, at the door, then entered". I imagined him as this lurky figure in a grey robe with holes for eyes – that's if he even had any. Thrice is a shuddery kind of word if you think about it...'

Vivienne drew closer to the fire, wrapping both hands around the enamel mug for comfort. Cocoa wasn't a shuddery word. Cocoa was associated with autumn gilding the trees in the hospital garden up the hill, hot rice pudding sprinkled with nutmeg, wearing shoes instead of running barefoot out into the early morning to fetch the cow...

'Haggis was another word that used to scare me,' Cathy said reminiscently. 'I imagined it like a jackal thing scuttling about in the mist and kind of wailing – like this...' The sound she made screeched horribly up a scale and down the other side, and the cat at Vivienne's feet shot away under the table, hissing.

'Did you know animals can see things humans can't?' Isobel asked, watching the cat with interest. 'They've got special sight. We used to have this old ginger tom and he'd sort of freeze and stare off into the distance with his fur on end . . . only nothing was ever there!'

'Bluey does that sometimes on the road up near Baroongal Flats,' Cathy said. 'He slinks along with his belly close to the ground and growls like crazy. Do you think maybe he's seeing something invisible we can't?'

'Tripe,' Heather said. 'That road's where Dad found him tied to a tree and starving for goodness knows how long and brought him home. Bluey just remembers someone was cruel to him there, that's all.'

Vivienne, rather wishing Bluey was home right then instead of keeping Dad company prospecting, glanced at the net curtains. Isobel was right – anyone passing by could look in at them gathered about the fireside, four girls all alone . . . Thrice could look in, things with cloven hooves . . . None of the others seemed troubled, however, and Isobel was offering to do Heather's hair in a stunning new style she'd seen in a film. Vivienne was sent off to find hairpins and side combs, but hesitated at the dark reservoir of shadows beyond the hall archway.

'What's the matter – scared of the bogeyman?' Isobel hooted.

'She thinks they're real,' Cathy said.

'What a sook! I gave up being scared of bogeymen when I was only five – I always reckoned they'd be scared stiff of *me*!'

Vivienne, embarrassed into bravery, ventured up the hall into Grace's room – although Heather hadn't let them call it that since Grace had gone to live in the city to study dressmaking. She'd moved herself and her belongings into that front room before the taxi taking Grace to the station was barely out of the driveway. Vivienne found the combs, but while searching for the box of hairpins heard something outside bump against the weatherboards. The sound stopped and didn't recur, but it was quite enough to send her scurrying back down the hall at a speed she had to disguise as diligence.

Isobel busied herself with the new hairstyle, and because the Mellings knew that she was a high priestess of such rites, they humbly accepted her judgement when it was finished. 'It's a waste everyone in your family being strawberry blondes,' Isobel said. 'None of you have the faintest idea how to show it off. See how I've improved Heather – it makes her look really old, seventeen at the very least, no kidding.'

'Three years older – really?' Heather breathed, and gazed contortedly into the hand mirror, trying to see herself in profile.

'I like it better the way it always is. That just looks as though she's got a possum sitting on her head,' Vivienne said abruptly, not wanting to think of Heather ever being seventeen and perhaps going off to the city as Grace had done. Then there'd be only Cathy and herself left at home – a home which might even prove to be a temporary one only, for there was some talk of the landlord wanting it back. Perhaps they'd have to rent a house even further out of town, for Dad still hadn't found work . . . Nothing decided, everything blowing about like dead leaves, Vivienne thought uneasily, hating change of any description.

'Drat!' Heather said, as the ceiling light suddenly flickered and died. 'It's not just the bulb gone – the street light's out in front of the hospital, too, so it's a blackout. There's no kero left for the lamp, either – Mum forgot to buy any.'

'Are you sure? She had it down on the shopping list when she went for the groceries.'

'She wrote out a recipe for a lady she got talking to on the bus, no prize for guessing what she used to write it down on. We're just going to have to put ourselves to bed by candlelight.'

'Candlelight and toast with dripping,' Isobel said. 'It's like a history lesson coming up to your house to stay. Not to mention an outdoor dunny, which is where I'm heading now. Give us the candle, Viv.'

'I need to go down the back, too, so we might as well go together,' Vivienne said quickly, wanting company on the dark lantana path with the night muttering so irrationally to itself. Isobel wasn't a very satisfactory bodyguard. She sped ahead with the candle shielded from the wind, and Vivienne stumbled after her, trying to ignore the inky night-time ocean of paddock spread all around. Isobel went into the lavatory first, taking her time. Vivienne waited outside in the drizzling rain, only partially protected by a chaff bag with one corner inverted into a makeshift hood, which she'd grabbed from the back porch. From the corner of her eye she suddenly glimpsed something, an unidentifiable blur which sent her leaping in after Isobel and slamming the door.

'It's not considered genteel to come busting in on people when they're in the middle of . . .' Isobel said distantly.

'There's . . . there's something moving about over by the water trough!'

'It'll be one of the horses or the cow getting a drink, stupid.'

'Dad's taken both the horses with him, and why would

Mona be getting a drink – she couldn't possibly feel thirsty in all this rain! Anyhow, what I saw wasn't that size, it was whitish and sort of . . . just floating around!'

Isobel got up and peered out through the little star-shaped window. 'You're nuts, there's nothing there at all. Making me jump and get a splinter in my *derrière* just for nothing – get a move on or I won't wait for you.'

'I'm finished, I'm coming . . . only you've got to go up the path ahead of me, just in case . . . '

'Course I will. Don't be frightened, I won't let any goblins grab you,' Isobel said kindly, but contrived to vanish where the path curved then leap out from nowhere croaking, 'Water! Water!'

Vivienne screamed and bolted inside where Heather was still examining her new hairstyle with a torch from her Girl Guide knapsack. She'd just come to the conclusion that it looked exactly as though a possum *was* perched on her head, and wasn't inclined to listen to any jittery stories about white shapes floating about near the horse trough.

'You're so babyish, Vivienne,' she snapped. 'I've got a good mind to ask Captain if I can get my Child-Minding badge just on the strength of having to live in the same house! In fact, the whole three of you are crashing little bores, and I'm going to bed. You'd all better go, because this black-out's probably going to last hours, but just don't keep me awake giggling and chattering half the night! Vivienne, don't forget to put the fire-guard up.'

'Why me?' Vivienne asked plaintively, but they'd already gone, taking the candle and torch and leaving her to find her way in the dark. The little back room was crowded with the extra bed set up for Isobel, who insisted on maintaining her nightly beauty program despite the lack of space. First she did some complicated bustline exercises, which Vivienne watched with amazement. She'd always supposed that bosoms just developed all by themselves without any assistance. This was followed by vigorous running on the spot, but Heather thumped angrily on the wall between the two rooms, so Isobel blew out the candle and got into bed. In the dark she slapped underneath her chin one hundred times to prevent sag, while she and Cathy conversed with each other in French. Vivienne knew it was only showing off because they were in secondary school and she wasn't, and even though it sounded as though they were sharing sophisticated private jokes, they really didn't seem to know very many French words between them. Probably they were just counting to fifty over and over, she decided, pulling the blankets up around her ears to blot out their affectedness.

The blankets weren't thick enough to muffle the weird noises sifting in from outside. Water gurgled in a nearby downpipe, normally a cosy sound, but tonight it seemed like a sinister monologue taking place out there in the darkness. That idiotic French conversation had been preferable, but Cathy and Isobel were now quiet and settling to sleep. Vivienne lay and listened with escalating alarm to other noises and their untraceable sources, a pattering, something clicking, a rustling as though all the fallen leaves under the poplar trees were being turned over, a thud . . .

She reached out into the dark and grabbed the nearest foot. 'Isobel – wake up! You've *got* to wake up, there's someone moving about in the backyard!'

'Probably only Thrice,' Cathy murmured drowsily.

'I expect he often prowls about out there when he's got nothing better to do.'

'Waving his stumps – did we tell you he's only got mangled stumps instead of arms?' Isobel said. 'Knock it off, Vivienne, if I don't get a full eight hours sleep I'll wake up with my complexion looking like baked custard!'

'You're both mean! I'm closest to the door and if anyone creeps in here I'll get grabbed first!' Vivienne whispered, twisting clammy hands together.

'No one can get in. Heather locked the back door, I saw her do it,' Isobel said with considerate reassurance, but added, 'although that's not really much use . . . '

'Why not? What do you mean?'

'The key's still in the lock. Thrice could just slide a piece of newspaper under the gap, poke the key out with a bit of wire so it lands on the paper, then pull the whole lot through to the outside . . . Though maybe he might find it tricky with his mangly old stumps.'

'Couldn't . . . couldn't one of you go out and look through the kitchen window?'

'It's *your* bogeyman,' Cathy said. 'You do it. Poor old Thrice with his flappy robe and his holes for eyes – he certainly seems sweet on you, Viv, the way he keeps following you around. Why don't you get up and make him some tea?'

'She'd have to hold the cup for him, though,' Isobel tittered. 'How would he hook his stump through the handle?'

Because they obviously weren't going to budge, Vivienne crept out to the kitchen window and nervously scanned what she could see of the backyard. Something gleamed palely through the dark drizzle, but it was only a suppercloth which they'd forgotten to fetch from the line. She demisted the glass and looked again, tracing the outlines of wheelbarrow, fowl-yard door, mulberry tree, Cathy's attempt at making a canoe – all reassuring stationary objects, and . . . a white *something* that whisked suddenly from under the tank-stand and around the side of the house, moving so quickly she saw it only as a blur. In fact, it had seemed to be a collection of somethings, all wobbling horribly about, then vanishing into the darkness . . .

She ran, yelling, up the hall into the front room and dived under the bed covers. Heather woke up and scrabbled groggily about on her bedside table, found the torch and switched it on with an expression that promised no good for anyone.

'I saw this thing out in the yard!' Vivienne whimpered through the crocheted holes of the Afghan rug. 'Oh, it was so *awful* – and it's still out there, whatever it is!'

'What's wrong with Viv?' asked Cathy and Isobel from the doorway.

'And just what are you both doing in my room?' Heather demanded coldly. 'What is this – matinée time at the Roxy?'

'We only came in to see what all the yelling was about,' Cathy said. 'She won't let us get any sleep. Every five minutes she's saying something's wandered out of the hospital morgue and come down the hill to tap on our window.'

'That really did happen once, kind of,' Isobel said. 'There was this patient died, so they bunged him in the morgue all wrapped up in a shroud with a bandage tying up his chin. But he hadn't really died, he was just in a coma. He woke up and opened the door and wandered about in a daze trying to find his way home ... You needn't look so superior, Heather, it happens to be true! That corpse blundered right into a meeting of the Hospital Ladies' Auxiliary and one of them fainted into the passionfruit sponge ... '

'That morgue's got a heavy padlocked shutter over the door from the outside – and I keep telling you it's not even a morgue, it's an electric generator,' Heather said cuttingly. 'Get your froggy feet out of my bed this minute, Vivienne!'

'There *is* something outside – I saw it through the kitchen window! If you don't go and chase it away, I'm going to tell Mum on you when she gets home! I'll tell your Guide captain, too, and she'll take all your badges off you! Guides are supposed to be brave and go in dark tunnels and things and rescue people ... '

'She won't give anyone any peace unless you have a look,' Cathy said. 'You know what she's like.'

'Please, Heather!' Vivienne whispered.

'If I do go, you've got to be my slave all next week and clean my school shoes. Plus give me the cream off the top of the milk when it's your turn, and do the washing-up when it's mine. And I'll expect my bike to be brought round to the front door every morning at eight on the dot with the tyres pumped up!'

Vivienne nodded mutely and watched her march out to the back door and fling it open as casually as though she were just going outside to gather parsley for a white sauce. Cathy and Isobel watched, too, as Heather went all around the yard, flashing her torch at the door of the fowl-run, into the cowbail and under the tank-stand. She tramped all the way to the end of the lantana path, then came back and gazed scornfully up at Vivienne on the porch.

'I just hope you're satisfied, waking everyone up when there's nothing out here at . . . ' she said, then stopped as abruptly as though a hand had been clapped over her mouth. She sprang up the steps so fast it almost seemed as though she'd achieved the incredible feat of covering all six in one bound, pushed everyone frantically inside and slammed the door.

'I saw . . . under the house . . . something white!' she gabbled. 'A white ghostly thing, sort of . . . quivering! Quick, someone, help me drag the kitchen table across the door for a barricade!'

'There's the front door, too!' Cathy squeaked, catching her panic. 'That loose glass panel – anyone could shove it in and reach through and unsnib the latch! Quick – the hallstand . . . '

They rushed at the heavy stand and tugged it, cursing each other for slowness, barked shins and stubbed toes, until it blocked the front door, then Cathy climbed on a chair and took down the heftiest sabre from Dad's collection of military swords.

'That's not going to be much use,' Isobel said. 'It might have worked okay for your dad swaggering around in that old war and biffing people – but this is different.'

'How do you mean?' Cathy asked nervously.

'If you poke a ghost with a sword, it just goes straight through, like slicing through air.'

'We're never going to let you stay overnight ever again, Isobel Dion!' Heather said. 'If any situation's bad, you always make it a whole lot worse!'

'It's all Vivienne's fault, really,' Isobel pointed out. 'If

*𝒥* 13

she hadn't been hearing things that go bump and making you go outside and check up, we wouldn't even have known there was a ghost on the loose.'

'That's not fair, blaming me!' Vivienne protested, but could feel their unanimous disapproval encircling her like barbed wire. She tried to regain favour by making an attempt to revive the fire embers, but accidentally knocked Heather's little torch to the hearth and shattered the bulb.

'Now look what you've done!' Heather cried. 'We'll just have to sit here in the dark because of you! The electricity's still off and there's hardly any wood left and the candle's in the other room. I'm certainly not going down that spooky hall to get it while . . . '

Whatever was under the house stirred. It pattered to and fro beneath the floorboards, whispering to itself.

'Oh, I can't stand not having a light!' Cathy wailed. 'Seeing it's Vivienne's fault, make *her* go and get the candle!'

Vivienne, bullied and nagged relentlessly until she gave in, crept along the hall to the back room. Isobel, she remembered, had left the candle on the window ledge. She groped her way forward, cracked her shins against Cathy's bed, and in grabbing for the candle managed to spill the box of matches all over the coverlet.

'Vivienne – you just get a move on!' Heather called.

She raked the matches back into the box, tremulously aware that the window was open a little way at the bottom. They'd been so energetic about barring the doors, but everyone had forgotten Cathy's fetish for fresh air even on the coldest nights. That thing from under the house could be gazing in at her right now, could perhaps fold itself into the width of a greyish-white hooded cloak and slither . . . Slowly, feeling as though there was no medal in the world magnificent enough to honour her bravery, she reached forward to close the window, but first, compelled by a degree of fascinated horror, put her eye to the gap and peered out . . .

She didn't go directly back to the living-room, but slipped into the kitchen instead and made herself a delicious corned-beef and pickle sandwich by candlelight. Then she went and perched on the sofa, humming airily to herself in between bites. Heather, in her absence, had managed to coax the fire back to life, and Vivienne noticed with interest how closely they all huddled around it, how they kept darting scared looks over their shoulders. They also gaped in disbelief at the sandwich.

'I just remembered something,' she said. 'Mum told us to get that suppercloth in off the line if it rained, but we all forgot. It's the good one with the pansy embroidery and if the wind gets worse, it could blow all the way up to O'Keefe's place, then we'll never get it back. I think someone should go out and fetch it in now.'

'Go . . . outside? Are you off your rocker?' Isobel cried.

'Go out *there* . . . after what Heather saw?' Cathy asked.

'*I'm* certainly not going out the back with goodness knows what on the prowl!' Heather said.

'Oh, I wouldn't expect any of *you* to do it,' Vivienne said nonchalantly. 'I can hear your teeth chattering from here. You don't have to worry – *I'll* get the tablecloth in.'

'*You*? You never go out the back by yourself after dark even when there's no ghosts about! I'd just like to see you going out to bring something in from the clothesline when . . .'

But Vivienne got up and dragged the table away from the back door, leaving enough space to wriggle through. She went down the steps into the blowy darkness, strolled across the yard to the clothesline and unwound the tangled tablecloth, then sauntered unhurriedly back inside.

'You can dry this in front of the fire,' she said, yawning comfortably. 'I'm off to bed now – though I suppose you'll be sitting up in here all night waiting for Dad to come home and rescue you from the bogeyman.'

'Viv, are you feeling okay?' Heather asked with concern. 'You shouldn't have gone out the back alone. I don't think you should sleep in that room all by yourself, either. Listen, what we'll do is stay together in here by the fire and just . . . '

'You can if you want to. If you get too nervous you can always call me and I'll come out and hold your hands,' Vivienne said.

She went to bed and lay listening to the whisper of autumn rain. She listened to the sounds from the living-room, too, the agitated whispers and small squeaks from Isobel, Cathy or Heather as wind gusts rattled the loose iron on the roof, or something banged in the darkness outside. The poor things were very on edge, she thought smugly, helping herself to Cathy's feather pillow and Isobel's soft tartan rug. They wouldn't be needing such things if they planned to sit up all night . . .

And in the morning, she thought, perhaps she'd tell them about O'Keefe's big white sow and three piglets which had got loose and now, after all their wandering about in various places, were cuddled up fast asleep underneath the bedroom window.

# ♪ A Gift From the Rajah

Heather, waiting dourly at the post office for a bus connection, wished she hadn't put her name down for the Home Visiting Scheme. She'd purposely chosen a moment when Mr Everett was standing in the church porch shaking hands with everyone – imagining him perhaps holding hers a fraction longer than usual when she volunteered. She'd thought he might even have said, 'I knew instinctively that you'd be the first young person to come forward – you put all the other girls in this parish to shame!' But it hadn't happened like that at all! Mr Everett, his distinguished silver hair shining like a halo, had just glanced at her absently and said, 'Oh yes, the Home Visiting list for the elderly . . . you'd better see my wife about that.'

The contents of her basket were also a source of anxiety – a dozen currant scones wrapped in a tea-towel, a jar of home-made apricot jam and two cakes of carnation soap. Heather had chosen all those things with care, but wondered now about the soap. Perhaps the old lady would think it was a hint that she didn't wash often enough – elderly people could be very touchy! In fact, she'd been

*stupid* giving up a whole afternoon just to impress Mr
Everett, and to add to her gloom, Isobel Dion came bouncing
along the footpath towards the post office making an
absolute public exhibition of herself! Other people, Heather
thought furiously, all seemed to have ladylike cousins they
could boast about, but she was stuck with that appalling
Isobel, who always dashed about town' in an eccentric
maelstrom of colour. She looked particularly noticeable
today, and Heather shrank back into the arched entrance
of the post office.

Isobel saw her, however, and shouted across the crowded
pavement, 'Heather, can I come up to your place . . . Hey,
isn't that Grace's old jacket she made out of the scorched
blanket you've got on? Dead clever, wasn't she, the way she
sewed fake pockets over the . . . '

'Shut up, you drongo! When are you going to learn to
keep your trumpety voice down?' Heather hissed, in a quiver
of embarrassment. 'And you can't come up to our place,
either. I'm not going home, I'm on my way to visit someone
over in East Wilgawa.'

'I wouldn't have thought you knew anyone over that
posh side of the river,' Isobel said. 'You can't count Uncle
Trip and Aunty Cessie, they're not really East Wilgawa even
though they like to let on they are. They're miles down the
slummy end near the old quarry, but wherever you're going
I'll come along and keep you company . . . '

'You will not! I'm calling on an old lady who used
to come to our church, Miss Bradtke her name is, and she
certainly wouldn't want a skitey loudmouth like you barging
into her house!'

'I know someone used to cook for the Bradtkes or do
their ironing or something. Old Miss Bradtke – she must be

about eighty not out by now, and I heard she's been one plank short, anyhow, ever since . . . '

'People start to fail when they get old,' Heather said reprovingly. 'That's no reason to talk about them with disrespect. I don't mind in the least giving up an afternoon to visit a lonely old soul who can't get out of the house much any more . . . ' She paused, thinking how thrilling it would have been if Mr Everett had strolled past at that very moment and overheard what she'd just said. He would have given her a special smile of approval, his lupin-coloured eyes crinkling up at the corners . . .

'Well, I'm glad it's you and not me,' Isobel said. 'What a lousy afternoon you're in for – sipping tea and chatting about bunions. Can't you get out of it somehow?'

'Of course I can't, she's expecting me! The poor old thing's probably been looking forward to it all week.'

'More likely she's so dippy she won't even notice if you don't turn up,' Isobel scoffed, but Heather shot past her on to the East Wilgawa bus and took a seat on the far side so she wouldn't even have to wave goodbye.

She sat down carefully, keeping her pleated skirt in order, because she wanted to arrive looking a credit to the parish . . . a credit to Mr Everett. Maybe, she thought, as the bus rattled across the bridge and negotiated the hilly streets on the other side of the river, Mr Everett might choose this very afternoon to make his East Wilgawa parish rounds! Naturally she hadn't picked today just because he *did* sometimes visit parishioners on Saturday afternoons, but what an amazing coincidence if he found her there at Miss Bradtke's being solicitous and helpful! He might even mention something about it in his sermon tomorrow, how he'd been so impressed by her charitableness he was holding it up as a shining example to the whole congregation . . .

The streets became unfamiliar, because she wasn't often over this side of town, but she checked the little map Mrs Everett had drawn for her, getting off at the tennis courts as instructed. Despite the instructions (what uneducated handwriting Mrs Everett had, and how *odd* that Mr Everett had married someone so ghastly) the Bradtke house was difficult to find.

It was tucked away in a side street where the houses didn't even have numbers. Heather walked up the long drive, noticing how neglected everything was, even though the house looked impressive from the stately front gate. The garden had probably been lovely once, cascading in a series of terraces down to the river, but now all its winding path-ways were nothing more than grassy troughs. She knocked at the front door, thinking that Miss Bradtke must feel ashamed to be living in such a rundown place, with most of the veranda tiles either cracked or missing altogether, and the brass doorknocker covered in verdigris. Perhaps that was why she was taking so long to answer, but when Miss Bradtke fumbled open the door at last, she saw that the slow-ness was due to extreme old age. She was a very ugly old lady, Heather thought, and just as decrepit as her surroundings in an ancient cardigan with all the buttons hanging by threads and slippers like collapsing sand-castles – but worst of all, she didn't seem to know anything about the Home Visiting Scheme!

'They said you'd be expecting me . . .' Heather faltered, turning pink. 'At church they asked for volunteers to . . .'

'Ah, a donation,' Miss Bradtke said graciously. 'Is it

for the font fund? They're planning to bring a special rock from Palestine, you know, to use as a base.'

'Er . . . they've already had that there for years,' Heather said. 'I mean . . . I was baptised in it. It's not a donation, Miss Bradtke, I've just come to . . . to visit and help with any little jobs you might need doing. Dusting and cleaning windows, things like that. Mrs Everett said she'd been in touch with all the people on the list and you're my . . . I mean I've been sent to . . . '

'Visiting? How splendid – I hardly ever get any callers these days! Come in, dear, let me take your nice jacket and hang it up on the stand. If you'd like to go in there and sit by the fire – I have a little fire going, because I do feel the cold so badly after India, you know, I'll make us a cup of tea. Through that door on the left . . . '

'I'm supposed to . . . ' Heather said, but Miss Bradtke was already padding off down the hallway and it seemed presumptuous to follow her to the kitchen. Heather went through the door on the left and immediately regretted her offer to dust. Every surface in the room was velvety with it, and the knick-knacks arranged along the mantelpiece appeared to be linked by strands of cobweb. Her mother's standard of housekeeping was such that missing items could remain lost for months, but this was unbelievable! She peered at something on a table that looked like a mossy rock, flicked at it with her handkerchief and discovered wax flowers under a glass dome. She flicked some more and the flowers gleamed as brightly as coral, but the disturbed dust had settled languidly on her shoes. Heather sat down by the fire, discouraged. There were so many objects and ornaments in the room, and probably that vague old lady didn't even notice the state they were in or even care!

Vague Miss Bradtke certainly was, for although the tray she brought in held a silver teapot as decorative as a crown, it produced hot water only, for she'd forgotten to add the tea. While she was remedying that, Heather set out the scones she'd brought, glad now she had, for the tray offered nothing more than very stale biscuits. Miss Bradtke ate neither, she was too excited about having a visitor. Like a child, Heather thought uncomfortably, trying to imagine Miss Bradtke as a child, or even a young girl, but finding it impossible. It was as though she had always looked as she did now, an angular old woman with white hair dragged back into a bun and long skinny legs encased in wrinkled stockings. The only youthful things about her were her eyes, which sparkled as though this ramshackle afternoon tea was some kind of party celebration.

Heather, with fourteen years' experience of being polite to elderly relatives, smiled and nodded dutifully through a rambling monologue about Wilgawa residents completely unknown to her. She suspected that they had all moved away or were now dead, but didn't like to point that out to poor old Miss Bradtke. It wasn't going to be easy to stem that torrent of chatter and get on with the small jobs she'd come to do, but even dusting would be preferable to sitting here numbed by boredom. And cold – for in spite of the fire, chilliness felt entrenched in the large room, a permanent feature that might loiter there all year around, no matter what the season.

Nothing about this visit had turned out as planned! She'd imagined a little artistic flower-arranging, perhaps sprinkling some cologne on a lace hanky for pitiful knotted hands that couldn't manage the stopper of a scent bottle, dusting the top of a piano and then taking her leave in a glow of virtue. And Miss Bradtke would remark later to Mr Everett, 'Oh, it was like a tonic when that lovely Heather Melling girl came to visit me! Such a charming, sensitive girl . . . ' But instead she'd be ensnared here for hours, listening to a flow of persistent starved prattle. She began to feel depressed, wondering if perhaps *she'd* end her days like that, find that the years had all fled and she'd become a dithery old lady, trapped by age and infirmity, with not a soul to talk to.

'No, Miss Bradtke, I'm afraid I don't remember when the Cleeses lived in Alma Road. I've never really known anyone of that name,' she said politely, and turned her bored attention to the ornaments on the table by her chair. She picked up an elephant paperweight, but replaced it quickly, remembering that it was rude to touch other people's belongings when you were a visitor in their house. Miss Bradtke could easily say to Mr Everett next time she saw him, 'That girl the parish sent here had such bad manners. Heather Melling her name was, and she didn't really listen when I was speaking, just fiddled about with the things on my little table!' And Mr Everett would think she was dreadful and never smile at her again with his beautiful lupin eyes that crinkled up at the corners . . .

'That elephant's one of my souvenirs from India,' Miss Bradtke said, apparently not annoyed at all. 'You might like to see a few other things I saved from my time there. If you wouldn't mind fetching that leather trunk from under the window-seat . . . '

Heather didn't mind, for India sounded vastly more exciting than ancient memories of Wilgawa. She even drew her chair closer to see better, braving a pungent smell of mothballs that erupted from the trunk, but discovered that the contents weren't particularly interesting at all. They were just the same ordinary relics that all old people liked to keep – buckles, yellowing letters, hatpins, gloves. They didn't even *look* foreign, she thought, feeling cheated, but Miss Bradtke's eyes sparkled in the firelight as she brought out each item. To Heather's embarrassment she even draped herself in a large silk shawl and swayed coquettishly about in her chair as though she were dancing. The shawl was patterned attractively with flamingoes worked in silk thread, but the mothballs hadn't been effective, Heather noticed unkindly.

'Oh – India!' Miss Bradtke said. 'It was utterly magnificent! I spent the happiest time of my life there. Enormous houseboats on the lake with mountains in the background, and the water so still, just like a huge mirror! In the mornings the little boats would come out piled high with fresh flowers . . . those beautiful, beautiful flowers! And the splendid dances and balls, everyone arriving in open carriages with hundreds of little fairy lamps sparkling in the trees. You wouldn't think so to look at me now, but I was quite the belle of the ball in those days, quite the toast of the regiment. Ah, here's something – my little gold locket with the emerald! I used to wear it all the time then, it was a very special gift from someone . . . you can try it on if you like, dear.'

Heather didn't know a tactful way to decline.

'Romantic – it was just so romantic, like living in an enchanted land! Father was always threatening to pack me back home on the next ship, because I was a giddy girl, you know, very wilful. I danced with a . . . rajah!'

Heather sat very still, listening, the locket swinging forgotten on its chain.

'My rajah with his dark eyes,' Miss Bradtke said forlornly. 'He asked me to marry him, but it wasn't considered the correct thing, you see, not in those days. Oh, I cried and cried! My father sent me straight home to Australia when he found out.'

'That's awful!' Heather whispered.

'They never even let us say goodbye properly, it broke my heart. Oh, I cried for months and made myself quite ill! My poor white face in the glass, nothing but hollows and shadows . . . '

'How mean!' Heather cried. 'They should have let you both . . . '

'But at least I still have my little trinkets and memories,' Miss Bradtke said. 'No one can take those away.'

Heather didn't move, her mind pulsating with the romance of it. Poor tragic Miss Bradtke – who would have guessed there was someone living in Wilgawa who'd had something so absolutely fascinating happen in her life? Proposed to by a rajah . . .

The mantel clock chimed, reminding her of how late it was, and that Miss Bradtke really looked very frail and tired, as though she should perhaps be having an afternoon nap instead of upsetting herself with sad memories of thwarted love. Heather stood up, offering to wash the teacups, but Miss Bradtke wouldn't hear of it.

'Thank you, dear, but I never allow anyone else to wash that good china,' she said. 'I never dare – I'm always so afraid a piece might get accidentally broken. But it was so nice of you to call, and I'm sorry you have to go. You must have a little gift – something from India, of course, and because that locket looks so pretty on you . . . '

'This locket? Oh no, I couldn't possibly!' Heather

protested. 'It's one of your . . . your souvenirs, Miss Bradtke.'

'I'd like you to have it, it's meant to be worn by some-one young, not tucked away in a dark old room. If you could just see yourself out, I'd be grateful. I haven't been very well lately, and that river breeze in the late afternoon is very cold to someone used to a warm climate.'

Heather let herself out and became lost again on her way to the bus-stop, unable to take her eyes from the locket – a gift from the rajah! Miss Bradtke had practically come right out and said as much. She, Heather Melling of Sawmill Road, had actually met someone who'd had a love affair with a rajah, and was now walking home wearing gold and emeralds!

Perhaps, she thought, discovering that she'd somehow wandered two blocks past the tennis court bus-stop, perhaps one day she'd travel to India herself! She could train as a nurse when she left school, go to India and help thousands of suffering people. She'd be a magnificent nurse – Captain had said at Guides that her First Aid reversed-spiral bandage was the best she'd ever seen! In India her fame would spread far and wide, she'd be summoned to meet the rajah of that area to receive a special medal . . . and he'd turn out to be the grandson of Miss Bradtke's one! She'd be looking par-ticularly attractive that day as she walked up to the throne of the handsome young rajah to receive her medal (because by then she'd surely have learned to manage her unruly mop of hair). She'd be wearing her locket, too, and the young rajah would suddenly say, 'How truly remarkable! My grand-father once gave a locket like that to someone he adored, but remorseless fate intervened and she travelled away far over the sea. He died of a broken heart, but now this little locket has returned to its original country like a talisman . . . '

The Wilgawa bus came and she boarded it in a dream, having to be asked twice for her fare by the driver. She wasn't even conscious of the bumpy trip back across the bridge or of alighting, and when she found herself standing outside the post office without knowing how she'd got there, she decided to walk home instead of waiting for a connecting bus.

When she went to India and met the rajah's grandson, she wouldn't have to walk anywhere at all. She'd be carried around everywhere in one of those palanquin things, and furthermore, he'd build an incredibly beautiful marble palace and call it the Taj Heather in her honour . . .

'Heather! That's the third time I yelled – you sleep-walking or drunk or something?'

Wrenched from her vision of pearl walls gleaming in moonlight, she blinked with distaste at Isobel perched on someone's lion gatepost in Slidemaster Street.

'I've had a rotten afternoon mooching round with nothing to do, but not as boring as you, I bet,' Isobel said.

'I had a very interesting time at Miss Bradtke's, if you must know. She told me all about her travels,' Heather said over her shoulder, hurrying past and not waiting. She didn't want Isobel's company on the walk home, wishing only for solitude. Gold and emeralds, gift from a rajah, and when she got home she'd have to find something suitable to . . .

'Travels? That Miss Bradtke's never been anywhere in her whole life, poor old chook, she was born right here in Wilgawa and never ever left it. Nothing interesting's ever happened to her, either . . . except there was something, this kind of scandal that happened once,' Isobel said, trailing around the corner after her into Alma Road.

Cathy had a nice glass box she'd won in a school lucky dip, Heather was thinking. Maybe she could be persuaded to swap it for something. That little box was lovely, with a spray of forget-me-nots painted on the lid, and was absolutely wasted on Cathy, who kept silkworms in it . . .

'I know all about the Bradtkes,' Isobel said, picking up a stick and rattling it along the paling fences. 'Because Mrs Atkinson next door to us used to housekeep for them when old Mr Bradtke was still alive. And a proper nasty old coot he was, too! He had poor Miss Bradtke waiting on him hand and foot all his life and never let her go out anywhere. She was already an old maid in her twenties, Mrs Atkinson reckoned everyone said that, but to get back to this scandal I was telling you about . . . you know those hawkers used to come around in the old days selling dress material and brooches and buttons?'

Cathy's little forget-me-not box would be ideal, Heather thought. The precious locket should be kept in something befitting when she wasn't actually wearing it. And she'd wear it only on special occasions – until she went to India as a nurse, then she'd wear it every single moment so the rajah's grandson could have every possible opportunity to see it!

' . . . just a skinny quiet little foreign man, and I don't mean foreign like Mr MacDurridge down the butter factory, but dark skin and a turban kind of foreign. Miss Bradtke was nuts about him! He'd bring her flowers every time he came to Wilgawa, and they'd meet in secret down by the river, holding hands and all that stuff. I wouldn't fancy having a boyfriend in a turban, it'd be like going out with a genie, but I guess if you're cooped up with a bad-tempered old devil of a father you must get pretty desperate. It even

got as far as them planning to run off together, but . . .
What's that you've got around your neck, Heather? If
you'd told me you were buying something at Woolworths,
I could easily have snuck in and got it for you without
paying.'

'What?' Heather said absently. 'Oh, you mean this . . .
Miss Bradtke gave it to me.'

'That stone's only glass,' Isobel said, losing interest
after one quick look. 'I know all about jewellery – my
mum's American boyfriend sent her some real gold dress-
clips shaped like the Empire State Building. That thing of
yours certainly isn't gold, you can see where bits are turning
green – I wouldn't be surprised if she didn't get it off that
funny little Indian pedlar when he came round to her place!
Heather, don't walk so fast, I'm getting a stitch in my side
trying to keep up . . . '

But Heather, walking quickly up the hospital hill,
hadn't heard one single word. As soon as she got home, she
thought, she'd find a scrap of velvet and line Cathy's box.

## ℐ Wolf on the Fold

'No long faces like old busted elastic,' Dad said. 'Mum's chuffed at the chance of dropping in to see Gracie on the way. She'll be back next week, and you've got *me* home to see to things till then.'

Heather, Cathy and Vivienne eyed each other glumly and re-read the telegram calling Mum away to look after her sick brother.

'Bit of luck I was here when that came,' Dad said smugly. 'Otherwise you'd have been Orphan Annies for the week.'

'I always think orphanages sound well-run and lovely,' Heather said. 'Don't take this the wrong way, but you don't really know much about housekeeping and cooking, Dad.'

'Nothing to know,' Dad said. 'It's all commonsense and planning ahead, like making the porridge the night before and not wasting time on fancy stuff. Take what I'm making for tea now . . . spuds baked in the ashes, then scoop out the guts, plonk in bacon and a dollop of chutney, can of peaches to follow – and Bob's your uncle!'

The meal, despite their wariness at having him home

in charge of things, turned out to be delightfully like an indoors picnic, and afterwards he played Five Hundred with them all evening, using the contents of Mum's button jar as betting money.

'I think it's high time you let one of us have a go at shuffling,' Heather said.

'Girls shouldn't know how to shuffle. It doesn't look ladylike.'

'Better than having the same person getting the Joker four deals running!'

'Cheating – *me?*' Dad said, examining the beautiful hand of aces, kings, queens and jacks he'd just dealt himself, but a knock on the door interrupted the game.

It was Dad's Aunt Ivy, and he immediately looked a great deal less pleased with life. She was the one person in the world who terrified him, and Heather, Cathy and Vivienne understood why. Aunt Ivy's eyes were like little blue Bunsen burner flames as they flickered from the card game to the bacon-and-potato plates left carelessly on the hearth. Heather self-consciously put the cards back in their box and tried to push the plates under the hearth mat with her foot. She wished that the room looked more presentable, for as well as the clutter that was always there, Mum had added to it quite spectacularly in her rush to pack and catch the afternoon train.

'I've come all the way down from Baroongal to lend a hand here even though it's not convenient,' Aunt Ivy barked. 'I know my duty. Got a neighbour to drive me straight down soon as I heard about Connie's brother being laid up with the pleurisy.'

'It's amazing how fast news travels around this town,' Heather said. 'We only got the wire ourselves just before

lunch. It's very kind of you, Aunt Ivy, but you needn't have
bothered. Dad's got a free week, so he's going to be home
looking after us . . . '

'Leighton? No one in their right mind would call *him*
responsible enough to be looking after anyone!' Aunt Ivy
said crushingly. 'One of you fetch my bag in from the
veranda and put it in Grace's old room. I suppose you've
taken that over, Miss Heather, but you can just move right
back in with your little sisters while I'm here. I certainly
don't intend sleeping on that old horsehair sofa – and would
someone mind telling me why there's a great pile of laddered
stockings draped all over it?'

'A whole week of being minded by *her*!' Heather
whispered, trying to find places in Cathy and Vivienne's
room for her hastily retrieved personal belongings. 'If Mum
had wanted her down here, she'd have sent a message. We
could easily have coped on our own, anyway, or gone down
to Isobel's. Meddling old bossy boots, she's just like in that
poem – "The Assyrian came down like the wolf on the
fold . . . " and we're the poor sheep!'

'Never mind, I expect she'll nick off back to her own
place soon as she tastes Dad's porridge in the morning,'
Cathy said.

But Aunt Ivy was up before anyone else and had breakfast ready on the table. It was like nothing they'd ever seen
before in their household – thin toast cut into triangles, a
boiled egg at each place, the teapot wearing its cosy, and
honey in the hive-shaped china container instead of a glass
jar with buttery dribbles down the side. The revolting oat-
meal porridge which Dad had made the previous evening
and left simmering lumpily at the side of the stove all night
had been thrown out to the ungrateful chooks. Amazingly,

he didn't bellow about it or even demand to know why the chutney wasn't on the table, though he liked chutney over practically everything including boiled eggs.

'Hurry up and finish your breakfast, girls, then get ready for church,' Aunt Ivy said, emptying the teapot before anyone could pour second cups.

'Church?' Cathy said. 'But . . . Heather's the only one likes going to church! We were planning to go fishing with Dad this morning . . . '

'Indeed?'

'Oh yes, he had this plan worked out. Viv and me were going to keep lookout down in the cornfield while he pinched Mr Sylvester's rowboat, and . . . '

'They've got hold of the wrong end of the stick,' Dad said hastily. 'I'm always telling them they should turn up at that little church more often and listen to the padre instead of larking about on Sundays. As a matter of fact, I'd come along myself and set them a good example – only it just so happens my suit's laid up in mothballs.'

'It just so happens you'll find it sponged and pressed and airing on the line,' Aunt Ivy said. 'I attended to it before breakfast.'

In church she knelt longer than anyone else, as though pointing out to God how she personally would have handled all the various catastrophes going on in the world that week. Vivienne considered that the hat she'd been forced to wear was one of them, imagining that everyone was staring at it and laughing. She'd been elated when no hat could be found for her, thinking she might be allowed to stay home, but Aunt Ivy didn't acknowledge defeat in any form whatsoever. She'd unearthed a terrible old sun-hat from the laundry and given it a quick iron, but in spite of that, its red polka-dot brim dipped up and down like a fever chart.

To take her mind off the hideous hat, Vivienne gazed around the church, at the light filtering through the stained-glass windows, the carved lectern with its polished brass eagle, and the gold letters above the arch which said 'Reverence My Sanctuary'. When she was small she'd never known what those words meant, but the syllables repeated inside her mind had always reminded her of the deep rich chime of an enormous bell. She looked at Mrs Robinson sitting importantly at the organ, and the snowy surplices and black mortar-boards of the choir. Anyone, even Heather, could look holy with an elegant silk tassel dangling over one eye, but red polka-dots were another matter altogether . . .

'Stop fiddling with your hat in church,' Aunt Ivy whispered, giving her a sharp nip on the arm. Vivienne sat up straight, feeling badly done by. If anyone deserved that pinch it was Cathy, who was playing with the alphabet game she'd got for Christmas under the cover of a hymn book. The alphabet game was small enough to be held in the palm of one hand, with sliding squares which had to be arranged in order, but Cathy was just composing rude words.

Dad, sitting next to the aisle in a glowering sulk, was obviously thinking them. Vivienne felt sorry for him, knowing how much he detested being forced to wear a tie, which he regarded as the equivalent of a hangman's noose. A tie, and instead of his beloved elastic-sided boots, laced-up shoes to go with the suit – he kept eyeing the shoes balefully as though his feet were being held to ransom. Vivienne suspected that if he'd had a pocket-knife handy, he might very well have used it to carve his initials on the seat in frustration. He hated being made to sit still anywhere, and brightened up only when everyone rose for the first hymn. Community singing was something he adored, and not knowing the words or tune to anything didn't ever stop him from joining in. His voice thundered out now, swamping even the choir baritones, and Mrs Robinson at the organ kept skipping whole bars to catch up with him. But in between hymns he returned to his sulking, and when the service finished he darted out of church before anyone else and made for the gate. Aunt Ivy hauled him briskly back and made him chat to the ladies she met once or twice a year when she left her property to come to town. Dad hovered on the edge of the little group, twirling his hat around by the brim and looking desperate.

Next morning, getting ready for school, it was Heather, Cathy and Vivienne's turn to feel desperate.

'Catherine Melling, you're certainly not going anywhere looking like a prisoner in a dungeon,' Aunt Ivy said. 'Come here while I plait your hair.'

'Only little primary-school kids like Viv wear plaits!' Cathy protested, but Aunt Ivy made a determined grab and manufactured two plaits as stiff as antlers. Heather, sidling hurriedly from the house, was called back and ordered to change her socks for the black ribbed stockings she loathed, for Aunt Ivy had apparently made it her business to know just what was the proper high-school uniform. Aunt Ivy also noticed the artistic wristwatch and ring Vivienne had inked on her hand last night, and the whole lot was sandsoaped painfully off over the laundry trough.

'There,' Aunt Ivy said triumphantly. 'You've got to get up early in the morning to put one over on me, I can tell you. Off you go, girls. And Leighton – you can just stir your stumps, too. I've noticed quite a few odd jobs needing to be done around this place, inside and out!'

Odd jobs didn't seem an adequate description, as they saw when they got home from school that afternoon. The broken panel in the front door had been replaced, the veranda steps scoured with a wire brush down to their original coat of paint, also the concrete path around the side of the house. They followed it, discovering other marvels. The sagging fowl-yard fence had been mended, the lantana cut back, there were new props under the washing-lines which creaked under a vast burden of drying clothes.

'My goodness!' Heather whispered. 'There's those flared shorts we haven't seen since last year and accused Isobel Dion of pinching! And look – Aunt Ivy's even made Dad hand over his riding breeches to be washed! No one's ever managed to do that before!'

'You can have a glass of milk and a rock cake, girls, then get changed out of your school uniforms,' Aunt Ivy called from the back steps. 'Tell your dad he can stop for a cuppa, too – he's whitewashing out the cowshed.'

There were more marvels inside the house, which sparkled like a waterfall. The scrubbed floors smelled of pine disinfectant, the kitchen stove was freshly blacked, every shelf lined with clean newspaper, the rocking-chair turned upside down and all the dust hooked from its curlicues, even the draught-stoppers had been taken from the doors, washed and hung to dry over the veranda rails.

Cathy greedily put a whole rock cake in her mouth, but scooped it hurriedly out, deciding that it tasted like ammunition. She felt Bluey's cold nose nudging at her ankle and was able to whisk the spitty rock cake under the table without being seen. Bluey choked and gagged, drawing attention to himself. Aunt Ivy grabbed up the broom and swept him down the back steps and under the tank-stand.

He crouched there sadly, his whole universe jumbled, for as far as he could fathom his sole purpose in life was to move in a small fixed orbit with Dad as its sun.

'Hurry up and finish, girls, I want you to get started on that room of yours,' Aunt Ivy said.

'Our room?'

'Your rubbish tip, more likely. I want that chest of drawers tidied out completely, all the walls scrubbed down, and those books taken off the window ledge and put back neatly in the lounge-room cupboard. I don't know what your mother's thinking of, letting you ruin your eyesight reading in bed! After that you can wax the lino, maybe we'll find out what colour it is.'

'It's not really *my* room any more,' Heather said sneakily. 'I don't have to help them, do I?'

'Satan finds mischief for idle hands – *you* can clean the windows in there, Miss Lazy. And Leighton, don't think you're going to be sitting there swilling tea all afternoon, either – you've still got that mail-box to fix. It's an utter disgrace having an old bread-box nailed to the electricity pole, and a mystery why Connie's put up with it for so long.'

'Dad *likes* that old bread-box,' Vivienne said indignantly as they toiled away in the bedroom. 'It's what they used as a mail-box when they married and it's been at every house they've ever lived in. How would Aunt Ivy like it if we went up to her place and started telling *her* how to do things?'

'Maybe we can get away with just pushing everything under the wardrobe and wiping over the walls so they look wet and shiny,' Cathy suggested, but Aunt Ivy brought dustpan, broom, dusters and mop to supervise their work personally. To Heather's shame, Lady Regina came to light

in the upheaval. Lady Regina was a peg doll living in a
shoebox fitted with silver-paper mirrors and a matchbox
dressing-table. Aunt Ivy upended it on to the floor and
demanded, 'What on earth's all this?'

'That's Lady Regina Lombardy – Heather made her
up,' Cathy explained treacherously. 'She's an adventuress
travelling around the world and it's supposed to be the cabin
in her private yacht . . . '

'You fibber, I haven't played with her for years!'
Heather cried. 'And it was Isobel invented her in the first
place, not me . . . Anyhow, I only do it to amuse Cathy and
Vivienne.'

'Rot, you never even let us touch her! That red wool's
her hair, Aunt Ivy. Heather crimps it up on wet matchsticks
and pretends Lady Regina's just gone to a beauty salon. She's
got a whole lot of strapless cocktail dresses, too, and Heather
reckons she doesn't even need a bra underneath.'

Heather made a red-faced dive at the scraps of satin
and the miniature stoles made from chicken feathers.

'Lady Regina's been engaged seventeen times so far on
her cruise, and she's only got as far as Monte Carlo yet,'
Cathy added gleefully. 'Heather says a handsome naval
officer's turning up soon and he's going to be Lady Regina's
Mr Right – or at least Mr Right until something richer and
better comes along.'

'I think you read far too many trashy books, young
lady, and you're far too old to play with dolls,' Aunt Ivy
told Heather severely, tipping Lady Regina and her
glamorous wardrobe out with the other rubbish.

Heather went out on a secret rescue mission after tea,
but the cow had trodden on Lady Regina and snapped her
in two. She stood looking at the peg doll for a few minutes,

knowing that Aunt Ivy was quite right – she was far too old for such games. Grace, for example, at the same age had enrolled in a correspondence course for typing. She tossed Lady Regina over the fence, feeling as though a link in a chain had been broken, then went back inside to an evening that was almost unendurable.

She and Cathy did their homework in unaccustomed silence without their usual territorial battles over table space. Vivienne, homeworkless, was made to help wind Aunt Ivy's wool. She wished that someone would invent yarn that came already prepared, instead of long, seemingly endless skeins that had to be held tautly on outstretched arms. Whenever she lowered her aching arms, Aunt Ivy, winding each skein into a neat ball ready for knitting, clucked in exasperation and said that girls these days were bone lazy. Dad sat gloomily by the fire, at a complete loss because Aunt Ivy wouldn't let him listen to his favourite serial which he'd been following for years. She claimed it wasn't suitable for young girls to listen to, and none of them liked to say that they, too, had been following it for years. At nine-thirty she made everyone go to bed without supper, for she didn't approve of snacks before bed-time.

At nine forty-five, feeling lonesome for Mum in the bleakly clean and bookless room, Heather, Cathy and Vivienne crept into the kitchen to comfort themselves with French toast and egg nog. Dad was there before them, claiming that he couldn't sleep either because the whole house reeked of pine cleaner.

'I'm not going to be able to stand that old lady wolf for even one more day!' Heather said, hunting for cinnamon to put in the egg nog. 'Everything's changed about and awful – just look in the cannisters for instance!'

They inspected the cannisters above the stove and found that each held exactly what the label on the outside claimed – flour, sugar, rice, sago and tea. In their collective memory such a thing had never happened before. With Mum in charge of those cannisters, you never knew just what you'd find inside – lost keys, ancient Rice Bubbles, fossilised lemon peel, bits of string saved to tie up plants – and once, Vivienne reflected, a little bird with an injured wing being nursed tenderly back to health.

'Five more days to get through!' Cathy said sadly. 'Dad, you reckon you once fought off a whole enemy platoon single-handed in the desert – why don't you just tell her to go home?'

'Have a heart,' Dad said. 'Aunt Ivy's a different kettle of fish. I've seen her wade in and bust up a barney in a shearing-shed with only a little rolling-pin.'

'In other words we're expected to just lump it till Mum comes home,' Heather said. 'Well, count me out! I'm inviting myself down to Isobel's after school tomorrow night and every other night until Mum gets back!'

'Me too!' Cathy cried.

'And me!' Vivienne said.

'That Isobel's a dingbat and so's her mother, barmy as bandicoots the pair of them! You don't want to camp down there . . . '

'Better than up here with Aunt Ivy.'

'Listen, you can't do this to a bloke! If you all nick off, there's only going to be *me* here to get picked on!'

'Better you than us,' they said heartlessly, but because he looked so miserable, they made him an extra round of French toast.

'Bloody woman, why couldn't she just stay up the river

and get on with her feud?' he muttered crossly, refusing to cheer up.

'What feud's that? There wouldn't be anyone brave enough to start one with her!'

'Old Mrs Gammon who lives down the road from her did. One of them won a prize in the Show for a cake ten years back and the other one reckoned there'd been a mix-up and she should have got it instead. Jealous, just like two squally cats, and they've been at it ever since . . . '

'What may I ask is going on out here?' Aunt Ivy said at the door, making them all jump. 'Leighton Melling, I'm surprised at you letting these children get up and ruin their digestions in the middle of the night – not to mention joining in yourself!'

'Me? I only came out to send them back to bed with a flea in their ear,' Dad lied.

They all gasped at his craven deceit and still weren't speaking to him in the morning. He *deserved* to be left alone with Aunt Ivy, they decided, but their personal escape plans came to nothing. Aunt Ivy spotted pyjamas and tooth-brushes in various school-bags and said she certainly wouldn't allow them to spend the night at any other house, *especially* not Isobel Dion's, while she was responsible for them in Mum's absence. And besides, they had to come straight home after school to give Dad a hand cleaning all the rubbish out of the shed. Heather, Cathy and Vivienne turned pale at the prospect, but Dad, oddly enough, didn't react, even though no one was ever allowed to touch as much as a roofing nail amongst all his years of jealously hoarded shed junk.

'I'll make a start on the shed right after breakfast,' he said virtuously. 'Been meaning to do it for months, really.

Oh, by the way, Aunt Ivy, you know that old feller Bert Gammon lives up your way?'

Aunt Ivy glanced at him with irritation. 'Naturally I do, seeing he's a neighbour. Now, about that shed – you're going to have to make a whole lot of trips to the tip. I counted four rusty old ploughs in there and what looks like a complete tractor taken to pieces . . . '

'I was having a bit of a yarn to Bert over the front fence before I did the milking this morning,' Dad said. 'He came downtown early to pick up a new sawblade.'

'I'm not particularly interested in those Gammons and what they do with their time,' Aunt Ivy said. 'When the shed's cleared out it could do with a lick of paint . . . '

'Bert said to give you his regards. Oh . . . and his missus sends hers and wants to know just when you're planning to sell up.'

'Sell up? I'm certainly not planning to sell anything! Why on earth would they have such a stupid idea?'

'Well, as far as I can make out they seem to think you're planning on living down here permanently. With us, to be close to the hospital. Bert says he was very sorry to hear about your ticker, but his missus wasn't surprised – she thought you've been looking a bit pale round the gills lately.'

'The nerve of that Agnes Gammon – I've never had a day's sickness in my life!'

'Aunt Ivy, I've really got to hand it to you,' Dad said admiringly. 'You're a real old battler, and even if you had double pneumonia you'd just pass it off as hayfever. You should have told us you've been crook, you know. Tearing around doing all the work here, it's not right, specially if the old ticker's mucking up on you. I don't think you should walk up that hill to the hospital for treatment, either – one of the girls can nick up there and get a lend of a wheel-chair . . . '

'I've never ever been to hospital and I don't intend to!' Aunt Ivy said with scorn. 'Illness is all in the mind. Why, that time I gashed my leg out in the paddock I just boiled up a needle and thread and stitched it up myself! Looking poorly, indeed – I can run rings around Agnes Gammon any old day! Gossip-mongers, that's all they are up in Baroongal. Leave that place for five minutes and they're all hard at it, ripping people's reputations to shreds! There's *nothing* wrong with my heart . . . '

'Well, I'm pleased to hear it. The way Bert was telling it, you wouldn't even be up to putting your cake entry in the Show this year.'

'Oh, won't I, indeed? If Agnes Gammon thinks that, she's in for a very nasty shock!'

'I'm pleased to hear there's nothing wrong with your health,' Dad said. 'They're a lot of blabbermouths up there, just like you said. I know what you mean about that Mrs Gammon, she sounds the type can do you serious dirt if you're not there to keep her in check. Take that other thing Bert mentioned, those little frippery icing things you put on cakes . . . '

'Just what *are* you talking about, Leighton?'

'Not me – Bert's missus. She reckoned to Bert you'll probably be buying a packet of those little icing things ready-made from the bakery on account of your arthritis. To put on your Show cake, if you can manage to get one made in time this year . . . '

'Ready-made cake decorations from the bakery?' Aunt Ivy said faintly. 'You girls – I don't know why you're all still sitting around when it's time you were off to school.

You're big enough to get yourself off to school without being stood over . . . and as a matter of fact, Leighton, I don't see why on earth you couldn't all manage on your own till Connie gets back.'

'I suppose I could,' Dad said. 'It's just a matter of keeping noses to the grindstone. I'll get on to those bone-idle hussies soon as they come home from school, make sure none of the chores get skimped. Too much larking around and frittering away their time, that's the trouble . . . '

'I'd stay a bit longer, of course, but there's a few things I have to get done up at my place. My little fondant icing flowers I make every year, got to get them just right. More than right – perfect. What time does the mail-van pass by here?'

'About twenty minutes,' Dad said. 'You girls, where's your manners, look lively and give your aunt a hand with her packing.'

'Dad,' Cathy said, cunningly staying behind to unbraid her antler plaits. 'You went straight out the back to do the milking this morning – I saw you.'

'So what?' Dad asked, whistling.

'So – how could you *possibly* have talked to anyone over the front fence?'

'Hold your gabby tongue,' Dad whispered. 'Or I won't let you wag school and come fishing with me.'

## 𝒥 Bridesmaid

'It's not really maroon and it's not exactly burgundy,' Heather said. 'Cerise, maybe . . . '

'Red,' Isobel said firmly. 'It's going to be the most peculiar-looking wedding – fancy walking down the aisle with four bridesmaids dressed in *red*! Bridesmaids always wear pink or blue or maybe at a pinch mauve, and if you ask me, Cathy's going to look exactly like one of those page-boys they have in big posh hotels. I wouldn't be surprised if someone asks her for a packet of cigarettes.'

'It's more russet coloured than anything else,' Mum said. 'I think it's pretty, even if it is . . . well, unusual. Autumn colours picked to fit in with the season . . . Hilary Melling always was a sophisticated sort of girl, so it was on the cards she'd choose something a bit different when the time came. Cathy's going to look sweet as a bridesmaid, and it's a shame Dad will miss out seeing her – though, mind you, I think he chose this week on purpose to go up and run the Grantbys' farm while they're away. He doesn't like weddings all that much. I remember when we got married, he tried to talk me into running off with him the day before so he wouldn't have to get all dressed up and make a speech. Cathy's the same. I just wish she'd show more enthusiasm, it was like roping a steer to get her along to the fittings even!'

She spread the bridesmaid dress carefully over the dining-room table beside the gold mesh Juliet cap, the gold basket and a new pair of red ankle-strap shoes, a gift to Cathy from the bride-to-be. Vivienne gazed yearningly at those glorious things, particularly the dress, which had been collected from the dressmaker that afternoon. It had a long skirt like a calyx, a square neckline trimmed with gold braid, and a beauty that magnetised her fingers.

'Vivienne, don't you *dare* touch anything on this table!' Mum ordered. 'And that goes for the whole lot of you – I'm going to shut the door and no one's to come in here at all. Heaven knows, I've got more than enough to do without sponging off sticky fingerprints and ironing out creases. There's my poem to write. I've never missed out yet commemorating the special events in people's lives with a nice verse – and you can't believe how hard it is to find a word that rhymes with Hilary. Plus there's all those little posies to make up yet.'

'Cathy's got to stand at the church door with the gold basket and hand out flower sprays to all the ladies as they go in,' Heather explained to Isobel.

'Well, if I was a guest I'd rather get handed a glass of champagne right at the start. And that basket looks more like a gold stingray . . . '

'Isobel, you can run along home now you've seen Cathy's outfit,' Mum said crisply, ticking off agitated lists in her mind. 'The girls won't have time to sit around gossiping, they've got to help me with all the last-minute things. The posies, plus all those chicken wishbones out in the kitchen waiting to be painted gold and have little ribbon bows tied on . . . oh, how I miss Grace at a time like this! It's such a pity she couldn't get time off for the wedding. Still, I mustn't grumble about that, she'll be home for a visit in a few weeks.'

'Grace is well out of it,' Heather told Isobel. 'That's another one of Hilary's high-falutin ideas, those chicken wishbones. They're for the table place-settings, and I don't see why *she* couldn't be doing it instead of us. She's the one thought it up. I don't think it's fair, anyhow – Viv and me have been slaving away collecting fern down by the river and stuff like that, and we're not even invited to her old wedding! It's only Mum going, and Cathy because of her being one of the bridesmaids.'

'Hilary had to draw the line somewhere. If she invited every relation in Wilgawa there wouldn't even be standing room,' Mum said. 'And where is that aggravating Cathy, by the way? I want her fetched in now from wherever she is to have her hair washed and put up in rag curlers – better not mention the curlers until you've got her safely inside.'

Cathy wasn't difficult to find. For the past week she'd been spending all her free time building a complicated platform in a tree at the end of the paddock. Furious at being disturbed, she scowled down at them with a fistful of nails.

'There's a scratch on your cheek going to need half a bottle of calamine lotion to disguise it,' Heather said. 'You're supposed to be a bridesmaid tomorrow, in case you've forgotten. Come down out of there before you do yourself any more damage.'

Cathy fingered the scratch and dismissed it as minor surface injury, nothing which she or anyone else in their right minds need be concerned about. She banged in another nail and inspected the result. In her imagination, the finished lookout would be as splendid as a military headquarters, boasting multiple levels connected by gangways, a trapdoor and a secret safe with a combination lock where she could store her possessions. But all she had to show so far for several days' hard work – maddeningly interrupted at intervals by stupid dress-fittings – was a rough floor of planks and a wonky roof, the seams filled with tar. Some of the planks creaked and wobbled alarmingly. Perhaps, she thought, it might be advisable to prise the whole lot off and try hammering them down at a different angle . . .

'Mum wants you right now,' Heather said bossily.

'You've got to come in and have your hair washed and put up in rags for tomorrow,' Isobel blabbed.

Cathy, enraged, hurled away the fistful of nails and yelled, 'I'm *not* having my hair tied up in curling rags and end up looking like a merino! It's bad enough I've got to wear that gruesome dress! I didn't even want to be a bridesmaid, and I don't see why they couldn't have asked Vivienne instead – she's so soft in the head she'd probably *like* it!'

'Hilary Melling's your godmother, that's why you got asked,' Heather said. 'Come on, act your age and stop making such a fuss. You know you can't get out of having your hair done.'

Cathy climbed miserably down the slats she'd nailed to the tree trunk for a ladder. 'I've got a good mind to eat a whole packet of prunes before I go to bed,' she said. 'Then they'd *have* to use Viv instead of me. There's only going to be one good thing about this whole rotten wedding, and that's the party food afterwards. Asparagus rolls, they're having, and little crumbed cutlets done up in paper frills and Napoleon cakes . . . '

'Make sure you pinch some off the table and bring them home for us,' Isobel said greedily.

'And just where am I supposed to hide them?'

'In your gold stingray basket, of course,' Isobel smirked. 'Geeze, what a hoot having to lug that thing down the aisle, just like Little Red Riding Hood . . . '

Cathy's foot shot out and Isobel sat down suddenly on a thistle.

'It's not polite to poke fun about people's weddings,' Vivienne said indignantly. 'I think a basket full of sprays for all the guests is a lovely idea. Cathy won't even be lugging it down the aisle, anyhow. After she's handed out the posies she'll be carrying a bouquet of gold pom-pom chrysanthemums like the other bridesmaids.'

'I reckon that sounds just as bad – they'll look like a handful of ox eyes on skewers,' Isobel said, and Cathy, plunged into deeper misery, stomped down to the house to have her hair lathered and rinsed in a basin then curled tightly around strips torn from an old pillowcase, with Mum ignoring all her squawks.

'I'll never be able to get to sleep tonight lying on all this!' Cathy muttered furiously. 'It's medieval torture, just like the rack – why don't you yank my fingernails out, too, while you're about it!'

'Fingernails – I'm glad you reminded me,' Mum said. 'Isobel, you can make yourself useful for a change before you scoot off home. Do something about this child's nails, they look as though she's been putting up dry-stone walls all her life.'

Cathy grizzled and complained while her cuticles were

pushed back and the nails filed ruthlessly into neat ovals. To complete the manicure, Isobel rubbed in cold cream and made her put on a pair of cotton gloves, with instructions that they weren't to be removed until the morning. Cathy, not in the least grateful, didn't get up to see her out or wave goodbye. She scowled all through supper, cheering up only when she realised that she couldn't be expected to do the dishes with her hands encased in beauty gloves, even though it was her turn. She also got out of feeding the hens and fetching the washing in for the same reason, and Vivienne had to do all those jobs alone, for Mum and Heather were busily assembling the buttonhole sprays at the kitchen table.

'There's not going to be nearly enough maidenhair fern,' Mum said worriedly. 'And I don't want to skimp on them, either, and have half the relatives getting a posy and the rest missing out. That could lead to all sorts of feuds. We'll just have to put them aside and make up some more first thing tomorrow. One of you can go out before breakfast and pick some extra fern, but right now we'd better get cracking with these wishbones . . . '

Vivienne would have loved to help with a fascinating project like that, but Heather, who also liked being artistic with gold frosting, said she'd only make a mess of it. The wishbones were placed to dry on matchstick supports while Mum cut up a roll of narrow ribbon for bow decorations, snipping the edges into V shapes so the satin wouldn't fray. Vivienne wasn't allowed to help with that, either, because everyone in the house knew she couldn't even be trusted to tie her own plait ribbons properly.

'Stop breathing down my neck, it's like standing next to a llama! You nearly made me cut this in the wrong place,' Mum said crossly, and sent her off to sweep the hall, a job

Vivienne loathed because of the coir matting which had to be rolled up and then replaced. She cheated by lifting the mat at one side and flicking the dust underneath, then unable to resist temptation, slipped through the lounge-room door to gaze at the bridesmaid things. Oh, the dress was sublime, in spite of Isobel and Cathy's comments! Aunt Ivy had a tapestry firescreen with a lion and a unicorn worked on either side, and a princess in a blossomy bower in the centre. That tapestry princess wore a dress just like this one – a beautiful maroon-burgundy-cerise-russet dress trimmed with bands of gold, and a little gold cap on her head . . . It would all be completely wasted on Cathy! Tomorrow at ten she'd go with Mum across town to Hilary Melling's place to be garbed in all her finery with the other bridesmaids. What an utter and abysmal waste, such glories for someone who never showed the slightest interest in what she wore, and whose idea of a good time was sliding down clay slicks at the quarry!

Vivienne went out into the hall and listened to the preoccupied activity taking place in the kitchen. There seemed to be some crisis going on there about gold paint not drying fast enough and the wishbones having to be transferred to an oven tray . . . She returned to the lounge-room and wriggled out of her jersey and skirt. The beautiful dress settled luxuriously about her ankles as smoothly as water, the little gold cap sat on the back of her head like an opened flower. She climbed a chair to look, entranced, into the sideboard mirror. The dress fitted perfectly, apart from being slightly too long because Cathy was taller, and she curtsied to her reflection. She was the Princess Madeleine, getting ready for a banquet prepared in her honour. Soon her ladies-in-waiting would arrive to dress her red – no, *chestnut* hair, plaiting it into thick braids entwined with pearls. Her hands (petal-soft because she always rubbed exotic lotions into them at night and slept in gloves) would be adorned with magnificent jewelled rings. Those hands would carry a basket of beaten gold, filled with nosegays to toss to the humble peasants. How beautiful she would look as she entered the great hall which would be ablaze with a thousand tapering candles, her feet shod in delicate red slippers . . .

'Oh, you wicked little hussy!' Mum cried and whisked Princess Madeleine off the chair, giving her several hefty whacks at the same time. 'Cathy told me she thought she'd heard you sneak in here! The very idea, touching the brides-maid things when I said no one was allowed to, and so help me, if anything's damaged, I won't be held responsible for my actions . . . '

The dress wasn't harmed in the slightest, though Cathy, hovering in the door to watch someone else get into trouble for a change, acted as though it was now creased with wrinkles, stained under the armpits with sweat and all the stitches along the hem jerked undone. Vivienne, tingling from the slaps, retrieved her jersey and skirt, but Mum said tartly that she needn't bother getting back into them, she could just take herself off to bed in disgrace for being so disobedient.

Vivienne went, sticking her tongue out at Cathy, and telling herself that she didn't care, she'd *prefer* to go to bed seeing they were all so mean about not letting her help with any of the interesting jobs. And anyway, at least she'd had the chance to try on that glorious dress, probably her only chance, for Mum had plans to remake it into a skirt and waistcoat for Heather immediately after the wedding. No one could take away the exhilaration of having been Princess

Madeleine for a few brief moments, but Cathy needn't think she'd ever speak to her again after tattling to Mum like that!

She pretended to be asleep when Cathy finally came to bed, though Cathy knew she was shamming and acted provokingly on purpose. She let the wardrobe door bang, pushed the window up noisily, then jumped into bed so that it squeaked on its castors. Vivienne lay still and kept her eyes closed. Cathy kept the light on for a long time to read, clearing her throat boomingly at intervals. Vivienne gritted her teeth and said nothing. Mum came to turn the light off, saying bridesmaids should get plenty of sleep, but Cathy claimed that no one with their head pinched up in a vice could possibly be expected to sleep – unless they had some Ovaltine. Which she couldn't get up and make herself because of her hands being tortured in slathered cream and gloves. Mum, too busy for arguments, fetched her some hot Ovaltine, and Cathy took her time about drinking it, making loud appreciative slurping noises for Vivienne's benefit.

Vivienne deepened her breathing into convincing snores. She hoped, when Cathy finally turned off the light, that the tight rag curlers *would* keep her awake all night, but Cathy fell asleep at once. Vivienne was the one who tossed and turned in jealous insomnia, praying for a miracle to stop Cathy being a bridesmaid tomorrow. That horrible Cathy didn't deserve such an honour! She'd done nothing but moan about all the dress-fittings, and when Hilary Melling had taken her into town to buy those matching shoes she'd disgraced herself by asking if she could have a pair of riding boots instead and just wear her sandals to the wedding. It would serve her right if she woke in the morning with her face spotted with chicken-pox! Or – she might develop a sudden attack of stage fright, working herself into such a state of jitters they couldn't possibly risk letting her spoil the wedding. Then they'd have to find someone else – someone nearly the same size as Cathy – to take her place! Dozens of things could happen, Vivienne told herself, knowing forlornly that none of them would. In the morning Cathy would put on the beautiful red and gold dress and go off to be a bridesmaid at Hilary Melling's wedding, and that would be that.

Vivienne fell asleep only when all the Sawmill Road roosters began to greet the dawn, waking blearily to hear Mum having a prodigious dithering panic all over the house as though she were the bride herself. Vivienne was hauled out of bed and scarcely given time to eat her porridge, then sent off to gather the extra fern so the buttonhole sprays could be finished.

'I'll need a lot, not just a handful of mingy sprigs,' Mum said. 'If you can't find any by the river, try the quarry.'

'It isn't *fair* – why can't Cathy go and pick it? It's *her* godmother being married, not mine!' And that was another injustice, Vivienne thought angrily – Cathy having a glamorous young godmother like Hilary Melling! She and Heather were stuck with boring Aunt Ivy, who sent them only a card every birthday accompanied by hectoring advice about how they could improve their characters.

'Cathy's under strict orders not to set foot outside at all this morning,' Mum said, impulsively changing her mind and ripping off the new veiling she'd just tacked to her felt hat. 'She's been told to sit quietly in the front room and not disturb all those lovely curls I just brushed out. Go *on*, child, I've got a million things still to do, the sprays, and this hat looking like a chamber pot, with or without veiling. Now I'll have to resurrect my navy straw instead – that's if I can even find the wretched thing after Aunt Ivy tidying away everything not nailed down.'

Vivienne, feeling distinctly martyred, went outside to search for more fern, having no inclination to traipse across to the river or all the way over to the quarry. She walked up the paddock to the damp little hollow instead, and even though the maidenhair fern growing there was pallid and sickly looking, she picked it all the same, hoping Mum would be too busy to notice. She didn't intend to trudge around the countryside while that spoiled Cathy was loafing inside doing nothing at all! As it was, she was probably risking her life. The O'Keefes from up the road all said there'd once been an old well in the hollow, which had collapsed and been filled up with rubble. Nothing the O'Keefes said was ever trustworthy, but in this case they could be telling the truth. The hollow always felt damp even in midsummer, and might suddenly cave in while she was standing there collecting fern – which by rights certain other people should be doing! She could be sucked right down into an underground spring and drowned, and then there most likely wouldn't be any wedding at all. It certainly wouldn't look very nice being held on the same morning as a tragic family accident, although Cathy wouldn't think it was tragic. She'd most likely just be full of glee at having an excuse to get out of being a bridesmaid . . .

Cathy – who wasn't in the lounge-room at all, but had sneaked outside and was now up in her lookout! Instead of going back to the house with the fern, Vivienne charged across the paddock to point out that other people could be malicious enough to tell tales, too, unless they received a grovelling apology. Cathy, however, wasn't alone, but was engaged in one of her fierce, long-running battles with

Danny O'Keefe, who was scowling up at her from the ground. Both of them looked dangerous, and Vivienne hesitated, not wanting to be involved. This particular fight, she surmised, was because part of Cathy's lookout stuck over the fence into the O'Keefes' paddock, and Danny had decided to make an issue of it.

'I don't give a brass razoo what you think!' Cathy was saying belligerently. 'That land under the branch might be yours, but you certainly don't own anything in the sky above it! You just try taking potshots at aeroplanes and see what happens – by law this tree-house isn't any different!'

'I know the law better than you, Melling!' Danny said. 'If trees poke over into someone else's yard, then they're allowed to cut off the branch. That's what I'm gonna do, saw off the branch and maybe your skinny legs, too, if they happen to get in the way – unless you let me up in that lookout!'

'You just try coming up here and I'll rip off your ears and use them as potholders!'

Vivienne suddenly recalled a book she'd read where the heroine had united two warring families by speaking gentle words of wisdom. If she could achieve that where the O'Keefes were concerned, life would become much simpler. The walk to the bus-stop in the mornings, for instance, would be less traumatic without all those fierce tribal faces leering from behind telegraph poles. And she'd be able to get modelling clay from the quarry safely, for at the moment the O'Keefes considered it to be their own personal property. Anyone rash enough to climb down the quarry without permission ran a menacing gauntlet on the way out.

'I don't think you should talk to one another like

that,' she said earnestly, stepping forward. 'It's not friendly. I've got a better idea – why don't you both sit down peacefully on the grass and take turns putting your side of the argument? Do unto others as thou wouldst have others do unto thee . . . '

They stopped glaring at one another and eyed her with astonishment.

'In fact there's no reason why you couldn't end up being the very best of friends,' Vivienne simpered, greatly encouraged, beaming from face to face. 'Neighbours should always be kind to each other. For example, you could take each other peaches if there's any illness in the house . . . '

'O'Keefes just nip in any old time and raid people's fruit trees without even asking,' Cathy said rudely. 'And if I was sick, Danny O'Keefe's the last person in the world I'd want to see! Except the sight of him would be a big help if I wanted to throw up and was having difficulties.'

'Who let *her* out without a straitjacket?' Danny O'Keefe said with scorn.

'If any of us have any problems, we should be able to go to a neighbour and know we'll receive help and comfort,' Vivienne persevered. 'Imagine what a beautiful civilised place the whole world would be if everyone did that!'

Taking advantage of Cathy's stunned reaction, Danny O'Keefe swarmed up the ladder slats. Cathy immediately recovered and began to stamp on his knuckles, but he managed to reach past and hook an arm and a leg over the platform.

'Get off!' Cathy roared, and wrapped herself grimly around his other leg like a boa constrictor, dangling in space.

'Please don't resort to violence!' Vivienne begged, wondering why her speech, which was almost exactly the same one as the heroine in the book had used with such excellent results, appeared to be failing. 'Oh please, Cathy, if you'd just sit down quietly and listen to what he has to say – and Danny, I'm sure she'd let you use the lookout sometimes if you'd only . . . '

Danny twisted his free hand into Cathy's mass of overnight curls and tugged sharply. Cathy bit him on the calf and they both tumbled, yelling, to the ground, where Danny conceded defeat. But before retiring across the paddock to his own place, he scooped up Cathy's tar tin from the ground and dumped the contents over her head.

'Don't come back, either!' she bellowed after him, dabbing at the trickles that oozed down her neck. 'Next time you want a punch-up, you gutless wonder, you'd better bring along reinforcements!'

'Oh, Cathy, just look at you!' Vivienne whispered, awe-struck.

'Doesn't matter, it wasn't hot tar, only lukewarm heated up over a candle, and I can always get some more from the hospital driveway to finish plugging the roof . . . That Danny O'Keefe – I'm going to fill a bucket with chook poo and keep it up the tree for ammunition. If he dares show his ugly mug anywhere around here ever again . . . '

'Never mind that!' Vivienne cried. 'The wedding, your hair . . . '

Cathy went suddenly quiet. She put up an anxious hand and felt amongst the curls which spiralled all over her head. 'Is it all that bad?' she asked soberly, examining her hand and knowing it was. 'Couldn't I . . . sort of scrape it off or something before Mum finds out?'

'Melted tar doesn't just scrape off,' Vivienne said. 'Remember that time you got it all over Heather's sand-shoes and even turps didn't work? Oh Cathy, what a mess! It's all matted together like . . . like squashed blackberries!'

'Maybe that little cap will cover it so no one would notice.'

'But it's not just on top, it's trickled down all over the place! You never saw such a sight, Mum's going to . . . '

' . . . murder me. All right then, there's nothing else for it,' Cathy said philosophically and began to climb the ladder into her lookout, prising each slat loose after her with the hammer so that when she reached the platform she was stranded up there. 'I'm safe for the time being,' she said. 'And I won't get bored, either – I've got plenty of work to be getting on with. It's not the end of the world, anyhow – you'll just have to wear that cacky dress and be a brides-maid instead of me. You'd better go and tell Mum.'

Vivienne, after a moment's reflection, altered her face so that her mouth turned down instead of radiantly up-wards.

'You've got a nerve expecting someone else to wear your repulsive dress in public!' she said. 'I was just thinking only last night when I tried it on how ghastly . . . '

'I know it's ghastly, and I'm really sorry, Viv, honest I am. But listen – there'll be all those nice eats afterwards to make up . . . '

'That won't make up for anything! As well as that awful dress, there's the gold stingray basket and handing out all those posies! Not to mention having to wear that terrible little cap and Isobel giggling outside the church – you know her, she'll probably bring along the boarders from the Convent, too, so they can all split their sides! You can't expect me to go through all that for nothing.'

'Well, when the wedding's over and Mum'll be too tired to murder me so it'll be safe to come down, I'll . . . I'll give you my pen with the glass handle.'

Vivienne chewed her lip, considering.

'Plus I'll sweep the hall every time Mum asks *you* to,' Cathy promised contritely, and Vivienne went dancing all the way down the paddock to break the news to Mum that she had a hemline to take up.

## ℐ *Glamour Girl*

The best thing about being chic in a little town like Wilgawa, Isobel thought, was that there was never any serious competition. However, because of her own high standards of glamour, she had to allow plenty of time to get ready properly for school each morning. The Convent uniform in itself was a formidable daily challenge. There was no remedy for starched blouses with floppy round collars and a tunic that looked like a sentry box, but something could certainly be done about thick black stockings. Isobel simply bought a smaller size and yanked them up as high as they would go, rolling the tops several times around her garters to achieve a semi-transparent effect. No one, she thought righteously, could possibly expect legs like hers to be hidden away from public view.

The pudding-steamer hat, which was supposed to be worn square on the head with the brim turned down, presented no difficulties. Isobel devised her own fashions – hat tilted jauntily to one side, crown dented like a stetson or pushed in to form a little trough, brim pushed up all around like a sombrero. Girls waited at the Convent gate every morning to admire her latest hat style, although none of them was brave enough to copy. Just as they were too much in awe of Sister Benedicta to ornament their plain gloves as she'd done, with green braid sewn around the cuff and a striped scarf to match.

Her hair alone, which according to school regulations was supposed to be kept neatly above the collar, required a good twenty minutes' work each morning. Isobel would have died rather than wear plaits or a bob, unlike her cousin Cathy Melling who'd actually rejoiced when most of her hair had to be cut off because of an incident with tar. Cathy claimed it simplified life, and didn't seem to mind at all looking like an eggcup cosy. Isobel, however, set her own hair in dozens of pincurls overnight, then brushed it out into a pageboy style after breakfast. It usually stayed clear of her collar long enough to pass roll-call inspection, but by noon she could feel its luxurious weight descending to her shoulders. The other girls, pigtailed and bobbed, would say enviously, 'Oooh, it looks just gorgeous, Isobel! How on earth do you get away with it?' The ability to get away with things was vital for glamour, Isobel knew, and not only in personal appearance. For example, some particularly fascinating item had to be found to take to school every few days. Last week she'd written herself a letter and read it under the desk lid until Josephine Guilfoyle noticed, then she'd torn it up and swallowed the fragments. Josephine had been frog-eyed with curiosity, and Isobel finally said, 'Okay, I'll tell you – only cross your heart and spit your death you won't go blabbing to anyone else . . . '

Josephine learned that the letter was from a Third Year boy at the high school, but as Isobel wasn't officially allowed to go out on dates yet, they were forced to conduct the romance by mail. She'd instantly told everyone else in 1C, as Isobel had intended, but there'd been an expensive aftermath necessary to quell doubts. Isobel had been obliged to buy a box of Winning Post chocolates and send it to herself by mail, opening the parcel in the centre of a dazzled group at recess. A note accompanied the chocolates, saying 'To my raven-haired beauty – with undying love from Roland', but it had almost ruined everything. Josephine had sneaked up the hill to the high school, checked over the fence with someone, and found there was no one at all called Roland in Third Year or in any other class.

'That's just my pet name for him,' Isobel explained. 'You can't honestly expect me to tell you his real one, we've sworn a pact of secrecy.'

Then there'd been the photograph affair, made necessary when class interest in Roland seemed to be fading. She announced casually during sewing, 'Did I ever happen to mention I'm related to Ginger Rogers?'

'I don't know how you can come out with big fibs like that, Isobel Dion, specially when you're cross-stitching a missal bookmark!' Dorrie said, shocked. '*No one* in Wilgawa's related to any film stars.'

'Fat lot you know,' Isobel said, producing a glossy black and white print.

'Anyone can get photos of the stars – you just write to that Odeon Theatre fan club thing. I've got one of Margaret O'Brien. Oh, she was so cute in *Meet Me in St Louis* – I've seen that three whole times.'

'You would,' Isobel said pityingly. 'Take a look on the back.'

Dorrie turned the photo over and read aloud, 'Izzy

honey-bunch, I sure miss you a lot, can hardly wait for when you come over here to Hollywood for a visit – we'll have us a swell time! Hugs and kisses from your loving Aunty Ginger. P.S. Fred sends his regards.'

'Fred Astaire, that is,' Isobel said, snatching the photograph back before anyone could notice the writing was in green ink, just like her history essay.

That had been a very successful venture, everyone crawling to her like mad, and today she had something else with a great deal of potential. She set off for school down Tavistell Street, in the opposite direction to all the kids heading up the hill to the high school. That was a sore point. She longed to go there with Heather and Cathy Melling – not to mention all those gorgeous boys – but Mum hadn't budged an inch. Isobel often wondered glumly how she was going to manage being stuck at the Convent till she turned fifteen and could leave school for ever. The only consolation was that she was the sole person there with any glamour and everyone knew it, including Sister Benedicta. She stopped to grab a handful of late-flowering roses from someone's front garden, because it was always wise to start the week on the right side of Sister B.

At the Convent gate the usual cluster of girls waited to see how she'd be wearing her hat this morning. They weren't disappointed; today she'd coaxed the brim into a tricorn, and as she went through the gate she hoisted her skirt, too, allowing everyone a glimpse of the blue satin garter, her item of interest for today. She'd sat up half the night making it.

'Oooh, Isobel!' they cried. 'Where'd you get that – it's marvellous!'

'Elastic garters might be okay for the rest of you, but

I'm fussy about my lingerie,' Isobel said loftily. 'It's from Paris.'

'You mean Paris in France?'

'Where else? I know a lady who dances the cancan in the *Folies Bergère* and she sent it to me specially. And if Sister decides to make sure everyone's wearing navy knickers today, I'll just tell her I cut my leg and it's a tourniquet . . . Oh, good morning, Sister! These flowers are for you, I know how much you like white roses. They're my favourite, too – so pure and holy looking.'

Sister Benedicta, coming out to take Assembly, eyed her cynically, but said, 'Thank you, child, that's a very nice thought.'

News of the garter spread rapidly. Straight after Assembly Kathleen Dunkling from Fifth Year offered her half a Violet Crumble bar and asked if she could borrow the Paris garter next Saturday night. Isobel nodded obligingly. It was always advisable to curry favour with anyone in Fifth Year, even without Violet Crumble bars. She bounced gaily into 1C's class-room, risking a few casual fox-trot steps so everyone would think to themselves, 'That's because of having Ginger Rogers for an aunt and knowing someone who's in the *Folies Bergère* – dancing's in her blood.'

Sister Benedicta asked crisply if she had a nail in her shoe, and told her to sit down and take out her geometry text book. Geometry was a subject Isobel couldn't see the slightest point in whatsoever. It was a complete waste of time for anyone glamorous. She knew that when she moved to Hollywood the only mathematics in her life would be checking fat numbers in film contracts, and she'd probably have an agent to do that for her, anyhow. Besides, Esme

Tyler in the desk across the aisle could be relied upon to supply geometry answers. She'd seen every Ginger Rogers film ever made, and since the photograph, had practically licked Isobel's shoes every time they met in the corridor.

There was a flurry of noise out in the corridor now, of someone walking past the door, opening the one into the cloakroom, coming back to knock loudly at theirs and opening it before Sister even had the chance to say, 'Come in'.

'Am I in the right place, is this 1C?' someone asked. 'They told me at the office to come straight over. I'm new – my name's Paulette Makepiece.'

It was as though a large bright parrot had fluttered lazily into 1C, for Paulette Makepiece, astoundingly, wasn't in school uniform. She wore an emerald skirt and a red blouse fastened with a poodle brooch. The poodle had a little collar set with sparkling green stones. Isobel stared at it covetously, then noticed something else and almost swallowed her pencil eraser in indignation. Apart from herself, there was going to be another person in 1C now who had a . . . figure!

'Yes, I was told to expect you,' Sister Benedicta said. 'But surely it's been explained that uniform is compulsory? If you haven't been able to buy ours yet, you must wear the one from your last school until you do.'

'Oh yes, Sister, I know! I'm really sorry to turn up dressed like this, but we only just arrived in town and most of our stuff's still packed away in storage.'

Paulette Makepiece had a beguiling smile, with teeth as white and even as piano keys. Isobel noticed crossly that Sister Benedicta was smiling creakily back, something that had never been known to happen before where new girls were concerned. Paulette was given the spare desk next to Esme, and all through Geometry and French, the whole class kept turning around to stare at her. There was something about her personality which dominated the room, and Isobel, peeping with the others, simmered with jealousy. Paulette achieved that dominance with little effort, for she certainly wasn't brainy. She didn't seem to know anything about anything, let alone the future tense of *avoir*, but being dumb didn't faze her in the slightest. She just sat there blinking her enormous golden eyes under her tawny fringe, as regal and compelling as a lioness on a rock.

When the bell rang for recess Isobel leant across the aisle and said quickly, 'You wouldn't want to hang about with any of the others, they're just a lot of boring little twerps. I'll show you around if you like. I'm related to Ginger Rogers, you know . . . '

But the new girl didn't hear, she was being assailed by Josephine clamouring to show her where the toilets were, Dorrie offering her a lamington and the others shoving in where they could. Paulette smiled amiably at them all and allowed herself to be escorted outside where she was given the best seat at the base of Saint Joseph's statue. Isobel followed, stiff with resentment. That stone bench was rightfully *hers*, the place where she always sat to dole out expert advice on eyebrow-shaping and how to make your bust look bigger! But now this . . . *interloper* was enthroned there, with Josephine, Dorrie, Esme and half a dozen others gobbling up her every word as though they were peppermint creams!

'We're staying at that big hotel near the river till we find a house,' Paulette was saying, and the girls gazed at her, enthralled. They'd never known anyone who'd actually stayed in a hotel, specially not the impressive River Hotel with its arched double-storeyed veranda and the two trees at its entrance trimmed into the shapes of a kangaroo and emu. Isobel started to boast that she'd personally been inside that hotel tons of times because her mum worked there, but changed her mind. There could be, she reflected abruptly, a sizeable gulf between someone who made up beds and waited on tables, and the people who paid for such services.

'Dad's going to be buying a shop here, probably a milk bar,' Paulette said. 'Maybe I'll let you all come in and get free lime spiders after school sometimes.'

The girls drew closer, adoring, never having met anyone whose father owned a milk bar.

'And he's got plans about turning one end into a hamburger counter.'

Hamburgers – Wilgawa had never known anything so exotic!

'Have a fairy cake,' Josephine gushed. 'It's a bit squashy, but it's got lots of jam in it. Where's your father's shop going to be, is it that empty one next to the post office?'

'He hasn't decided yet. They're still looking around, and I wanted to go and look with them, but Mum didn't want me missing any more school. So that's why I've started already even though I haven't got the uniform yet. We didn't think it would matter in a little hick town like this.'

Such was her allure that no one even minded Wilgawa being referred to as a little hick town.

'I just love your swirly skirt and the cute poodle brooch with the little glittery collar!' Dorrie said.

'This old thing, you mean? Why, I've had it so long I'm bored with it now. I've got an uncle who sells costume jewellery, and he's always giving me brooches and things.

You could say I'm a bit spoiled, really – Dad even had to buy me a jewel box with a whole lot of extra compartments. Soon as we find a house they're going to get me one of those four-poster beds, too, with a canopy.'

'Wow!' Esme said. 'A four-poster bed with a canopy...'

It was about time, Isobel decided grimly, that a stop was put to all this. She elbowed Josephine aside and said, 'I'm Isobel Dion, in case you don't know. I can play the piano accordion and I learn tap-dancing, ballet, character and folk. As a matter of fact I'm related to...'

'There's the bell,' Esme interrupted rudely. 'It's Sister Benedicta again and we're doing the solar system, Paulette, but just sing out if you get stuck.'

Paulette knew nothing about the planets and didn't seem to care in the least. Sister Benedicta, however, told her that tomorrow she must bring all her work from her previous school so someone could assess just what she did know – as well as getting a uniform from somewhere.

'Yes, Sister, of course. I'll get all my books and school stuff out tonight,' Paulette said respectfully. 'Mum's been too busy to unpack, that's all.'

But at lunch-time she confided to Josephine and whoever else chose to listen, 'I can't really be bothered unpacking, specially when we'll be moving out of that hotel soon as we find a house. I *hate* school uniforms, anyway. Tomorrow I think I might just wear my midnight-blue velveteen pinafore, and the silly old crow can flap as much as she likes.'

Silly old crow – no one had ever dared call Sister Benedicta that before, even behind her back! The girls, mesmerised, squabbled with each other for the honour of sitting next to Paulette for lunch, and at the end of the day followed her devotedly down Tavistell Street to the bus-stop, even though half of them didn't usually go home that way. They looked, Isobel decided angrily, like paper-clips attached to a magnet.

She trudged home and didn't even glance at herself automatically in the kitchen mirror as she went inside, but just slumped at the table. Mum was getting ready for work, ironing the ruffled muslin apron which had 'River Hotel' embroidered on the bosom, and her tight black dress. Isobel had always considered that uniform rather stylish, but now had second thoughts. Perhaps Paulette Makepiece would sit arrogantly in the dining-room of the River Hotel and see it only as a symbol of inferiority.

'The old pub's just about bursting at the seams this week,' Mum said, smoothing the band of her starched white cap. 'I mightn't get home till all hours if they need help in the kitchen later. Make sure you get your homework done – and don't go making a beeline to my dressing-table the minute I'm half-way out the door, either.'

'Got to have something to do, haven't I?' Isobel said moodily. 'Seeing I'm stuck here all alone just about every evening with you tearing off to work.'

'Oh, love, don't be like that,' Mum said with sudden concern. 'Look, I know it's tough on you, but I've got to do the extra time with Vi being away. She always fills in for me when I ask her, and besides – where else can I get a job? I'm a bit long in the tooth to be an usherette again. You've always been such a good kid, not whingeing when I have to do extra shifts. I suppose if you're bored you could go up and stay the night at Aunty Connie's – though maybe it's better not to for the time being.'

'They never mind me going up there. Viv and Cathy said so.'

'They're too young to understand how crook things are. Poor old Connie's got enough on her plate with himself being out of work, plus maybe having to shift out of Sawmill Road after June. Goodness only knows where else the poor things can go . . . '

'I'll be all right staying home by myself,' Isobel muttered. 'I'll survive. It's just that *some* people my age live really different lives. Some people have naturally curly hair and velveteen pinafores and rich dads who own milk bars and uncles who keep giving them jewellery every five minutes . . . '

'If all that's a build-up to asking if I'll shout you one of those new season shorty coats in Osborne's, you can just forget it,' Mum said. 'I'm off now – don't let me catch you still up when I get home.'

Isobel was too depressed to contemplate anything but an early night. She lit the chip heater and ran a bath, throwing in a handful of Lux flakes to make bubbles. Paulette, she thought bitterly, wouldn't be feeding an antiquated bath heater with woodchips, she'd be splashing around in one of the ferry-sized tubs at the River Hotel, where the mirrors were etched with dolphins and the fluffy towels were as soft as clover. But she didn't want to think about Paulette Makepiece any more today.

She painted her toenails as brilliantly as orchids, which made her feel slightly better, and propped her feet up against the tap while the varnish dried. The sight of her school tunic on a nearby chair brought fresh discouragement. It was sheer cruelty making kids (especially ones with chic) wear clothes like that every day. There was no reason why school tunics had to be so unflattering, and someone should write a letter about it to the Prime Minister. Paulette Watch-

Me-Everyone-Makepiece had the right idea. Probably she'd get away with not wearing a uniform for weeks, just by using the excuse that her mother hadn't got around to unpacking her old one yet. Tomorrow she'd turn up in a midnight-blue velveteen pinafore and for the second day running look like the greatest show on earth.

Isobel eyed her school tunic with frustrated loathing, knowing she couldn't improve it in any way, even shortening it radically before tomorrow. Sister Benedicta quite often had tunic blitzes and was quite capable of ripping too-short hemline stitching undone on the spot. The victim had to slink around school all day in a tunic that flapped half-way down her shins and walk home like that, too. Tomorrow, Isobel thought dolefully, she'd have no choice but to be one of the paperclips clinging to Paulette Makepiece's magnet, unless . . .

She reached out and pulled the tunic into the bathtub with her.

In the morning she was specially considerate about not waking her mother, who had arrived home very late. She dressed carefully and set off down Tavistell Street, but her pace slowed as she approached the Convent gates. There was the usual crowd going in, girls with hats at the correct prissy angle, their skinny legs in black stockings like sticks of liquorice. Isobel raised her chin pugnaciously, telling herself that Sister Benedicta probably only yelled at people so loudly and so often to keep her voice in trim for the choir. And besides, she wouldn't be the only one out of school uniform today – she and Paulette Makepiece would be the stars of the day together, the only two people with glamour. Sister couldn't very well go mad at one and not the other, but in spite of thinking all that, it required great reserves of bravery to get herself in through the Convent gates.

'Crikey!' Josephine and Dorrie whispered, staring at Isobel's mother's tight black skirt with the slit, the crocodile-skin shoes and V-necked electric-pink angora sweater adorned with large dress-clips.

'If you're wondering where I got these dress-clips, Ginger Rogers – my Aunt Ginger, that is, sent them to me from New York . . . ' Isobel said, but her voice choked to a stop.

Paulette Makepiece had just come in through the gate, and Paulette wasn't wearing a midnight-blue velveteen pinafore at all. She was in school uniform, and not the stodgy Convent one, either, but an elegant tan pleated skirt, a matching blazer with a magnificent crested pocket, and a smart little beret.

'Oh, do you really like it?' she cooed at all the people who immediately deserted Isobel and thronged about her in admiration. 'It's just what we wore at this boarding-school I went to before we moved. Mum wanted me to stay on there but I didn't like it much, they were too strict . . . '

'Boarding-school!' cried Josephine, Dorrie and Esme, who were smitten with boarding-school stories that term. 'Oh, you lucky, lucky, *lucky* thing!'

'*Isobel Dion!*' called Sister Benedicta from the office window. 'You come here right this minute, young lady!'

'My tunic accidentally fell in the bath and I had nothing else to wear,' Isobel gabbled, trying to stand her ground unflinchingly but not succeeding. Sister Benedicta's stringent lecture about what was suitable and what was not to wear to school in an emergency like stupidly letting your tunic fall into a bath was enough to wilt even the tallest poppy. The Empire State Building dress-clips were confiscated and so were the crocodile-skin shoes. Sister Benedicta produced a pair of hideous sandshoes from the lost property cupboard, also a large handkerchief which she made Isobel pin into the V-neckline of the angora sweater.

No comfort was to be found afterwards, either, the others were too busy listening breathlessly to Paulette Makepiece's glittering anecdotes about boarding-school life. For the second day in a row Isobel suffered the cataclysmic experience of being practically ignored. Hardly anyone spoke to her at all except to say insulting things like, 'You look kind of stupid dressed up like a dog's dinner for school. And how come you're wearing your mum's clothes – I've seen her down the street in those things!' The maimed hours limped by. Several people complained that fluff from the angora sweater was making them sneeze and Sister Benedicta made Isobel put on a weird black cape borrowed from a postulant at the Convent. Everyone giggled when she went out into the playground like that, so she hid behind the statue of Saint Joseph and watched Paulette Makepiece swanning around in her wonderful boarding-school uniform like someone out of an Angela Brazil book.

When school finished she gloomed home and climbed in through the bedroom window to change, an act of furtiveness that wasn't even necessary, for Mum wasn't in. There was a note on the kitchen table which said, 'Never rains but it pours! As well as Vi still away, one of the other girls sprained her ankle, so now yours truly has an extra afternoon shift. What a life – never mind, maybe I'll meet a rich travelling salesman. Irish stew in pot on stove, I'll be home about tennish, love, Mum. P.S. You wouldn't happen to know anything about my pink fuzzy wuzzy sweater, would you, madam?'

Isobel felt too miserable for Irish stew. Paulette, she thought, would probably be having roast beef and the River Hotel's luscious Tuesday night dessert, pear and ginger tart, for dinner. Paulette . . . she contemplated a future so grim it made her eyes water. The best thing about the small pond of Wilgawa was that she, Isobel Dion, had always been the most noticeable frog in it, but now she'd been reduced to tadpole size – and she didn't see how she could possibly bear it! From now on great big glamorous Paulette Makepiece would be stealing every ray of limelight in every part of town – the picture theatre, Main Street, church, everywhere!

Isobel dolefully fetched her school tunic in from the line and pressed it, then ironed the brim of her school hat back into the regulation shape. There seemed little point in trying to look fascinatingly different tomorrow or any other day, Paulette would always be there upstaging her. And it would be even worse when her father opened that milk bar and hamburger shop – she'd radiate even more glory! Perhaps there was a solution: if the Mellings moved further out of town to Baroongal Flats or somewhere like that, she could persuade Mum to let her go and live with them. It was a dismal prospect, but at least up there she could go to that little bush school where there was absolutely no competition at all! One thing was certain, she couldn't endure living in the same town as Paulette Makepiece and face each day being a . . . nobody!

She was still sitting in the kitchen brooding when her mother came home at ten. Mum tutted about the uneaten Irish stew still in its saucepan. She'd brought home three wedges of leftover pear and ginger tart, but Isobel turned her nose up at that, too. Mum inspected her closely and said, 'I hope you're not coming down with the flu, you've been looking a bit peaky since yesterday, come to think of it. Here, I've got something in my purse might cheer you up. Some of those guests are so blooming careless, they leave all sorts of trinkets behind and never bother to write back for them, either . . . '

Isobel, without much interest, watched her search through the handbag, remembering other so-called treasures left behind by hotel guests. None of those other things had turned out to be anything special – cosmetic bags with permanently jammed zips, a silver belt that disintegrated in a heat wave, a watch with the hands stuck permanently at either noon or midnight. Nothing could cheer her up, anyhow, ever again. Her whole world was as effectively shattered as though a huge tornado had roared through Wilgawa . . .

'These people left unexpectedly and I had to clean out their rooms,' Mum was saying. 'The boss was in a stinking mood, he thought they were booked for another week at the very least, but they changed their minds and left before tea. This little brooch was on the floor, and the other girls are inclined to be a bit grabby about lost property, so I got in first for a change. There – maybe now you'll leave my Empire State Building dress-clips alone!'

'You're supposed to hand stuff people leave behind over to the manager,' Isobel said primly, staring down at the little poodle brooch with its sparkling collar.

'Get out, that only applies to money and proper jewellery. No one's going to give a tinker's cuss about a brooch with the clasp busted. Probably they chucked it out on purpose because it's broken, but if you glue a little gold safety-pin on the back it'll be good as new.'

'Who . . . who was booked into the room where you found it?'

'A couple with a kid, they had the big veranda room and the single next to it. I never had much chance to natter to them, though, we've been that rushed off our feet. The boss reckoned they were thinking about taking over that empty shop next to the post office, but they decided to buy a general store way down the coast instead. Vacant possession or something, with a house out the back, so they've gone haring off down there and good luck to them. I'm off to bed now, and you can do likewise – but here's something else might perk you up. I earned a bit extra from all that overtime, so you can pop into Osborne's after school tomorrow and buy one of those red shorty jackets. Not that you deserve it, kiddo, but it might stop you pinching *my* clothes!'

'Wouldn't be seen dead in your clothes, people might think I was you,' Isobel said, bouncing up to give her mother a hug. 'I'll go to bed in a jiffy, Mum, but I've just got some homework to finish off first.'

She tore a clean page from an exercise book and after much thought wrote in a fancy script totally unlike her own . . .

*Dear Isobel,*
*It's a shame we never got much chance to talk*
*while I was stuck at the Convent those two days.*
*Those stupid gabby little girls were a real pain*
*hanging round like a bad smell and we couldn't get*
*rid of them. Still, at least you and me went out last*
*night together – that was a nice farewell dinner we*

*had at the River Hotel, specially the pear and ginger tart and cocktails. Wouldn't that girl with the cross eyes – Josephine Whatsername – be jealous! And the other one with the rubbery lips, Dorrie, not to mention that fatso Esme. (What clodhopper names everyone has in Wilgawa except you!) Anyhow, as we're moving down the coast and I won't be living here after all, you'll just have to come and stay with us soon as we get settled in. Dad reckons you can serve behind the hamburger counter any time you like. I'd never ask any of those other twerps to stay – you're the only one in Wilgawa who's got any real glamour or chick. This poodle brooch is for you as a keepsake, too bad if those drips get jealous when you wear it to school!*

*Ta ta and love from Paulette.*

*P.S. Give my regards to your Aunty Ginger and Fred – you're so lucky being related to Ginger Rogers!*

'Isobel, I thought I told you to go to bed,' Mum called from the front room. 'You've got school tomorrow, don't forget.'

'I haven't forgotten,' Isobel said smugly. 'I can hardly wait.'

## 𝒥 Lilith's Curse

'I don't know why Aunty Con bothers to keep any of it when it's really just a load of old junk,' Isobel said.

'They're Mum's souvenirs,' Cathy said touchily, opening an envelope that held four locks of reddish-blonde baby hair individually wrapped in tissue paper.

Isobel certainly wasn't interested in those. She pried her way through ancient hats, a cylinder that rattled but contained nothing more fascinating than mah-jong tiles, rolls of childish crayon drawings, and a bundle of yellowing letters tied with ribbon.

'It's all pretty boring, even these love letters your dad wrote to her from the war,' she said. 'Take this one – it's just one long skite about how many shells he's dodged and how many people he's clouted . . . Oh, my mistake, here's a part that's not about fighting . . . '

'What does it say? Is it kind of romantic?'

'Ooh, yes, real moonlight and roses stuff!'

'Go on – read out a bit!'

' "Connie love, if by any chance I don't make it back . . . " ' Isobel read in a poignant voice.

'Oh, that *is* romantic,' Cathy marvelled. 'You'd never think Dad . . . '

' " . . . I reckon you could finish clearing that block and take it over on your own. Don't let Trip diddle you out of it just because you and me aren't spliced yet. No sense wasting all the bloody hard yakka I already put in grubbing out those big gums. They were a fair cow, not to mention all that bloody fencing. Next time you're up that way, old girl, better check all the posts for white ants and . . . " '

'It's not nice to snoop through people's old letters,' Cathy said coldly, putting them back amongst albums of faded photographs, postcards, and a satin corselet that had once girdled a much slimmer, much younger Mum. 'There's a fur thing down here in the corner we missed,' she said and pulled out something that looked like a run-over fox but was actually a neck-stole. The fox-head had amber glass eyes and was lined with rich brown silk. 'Wow, I never knew Mum had this!' Cathy cried. 'It's smashing – look at the lovely brushy tail and dear little feet!'

'It's not all that smashing. They're so out of date only old ladies like Aunt Ivy still wear them.'

'Yes, but think what you could do with it! You could drape it over your bed for a decoration . . . or maybe turn it into a nice furry handbag.'

'*You* with a handbag?'

'I don't mean anything sissy, more like a dillybag you sling over one shoulder. It would come in handy for sports days, I could carry all my gear in it. *No one's* got a sports dillybag made out of a dead fox! When Mum gets home I'm going to ask if I can have this fur to keep.'

'Why should *you* get it?'

'Because I'm the one found it tucked away down there, that's why. I'll have to think up some clever way I can ask, because she might be mad we went through her box while she's out. But I bet you she'll let me, seeing it's just lying there going to waste. The silk lining's nice, too, just like that material men have lining their best hats. That'll be useful, that will – I could make a sling out of it in case I ever break an arm at softball.'

'It sounds absolutely ridiculous! Cutting up fur and silk just for a stupid bag to hold your sweaty old sandshoes and gym tunic . . . '

'You're only jealous you didn't spot it first,' Cathy said smugly.

'Oh!' Isobel whispered. 'Oh, my goodness!'

'What's the matter?'

'Cathy, put it right back this minute! Don't even *touch* it – I just remembered what that thing is! It was . . . it was Aunt Lilith's!'

'Who? We haven't got an Aunt Lilith . . . '

'Well, she was your dad's great-great-aunt, really, years and years ago before any of us were even born. Cathy, I'm telling you, put it away and don't ever touch it again, not even with the fire tongs! Geeze, if you knew what I know you wouldn't be thinking about making it up into a purse or anything – you'd be rushing off to soak your hands in Lysol!'

'Why? It's perfectly clean, just a bit dusty, that's all . . . '

'I'm not talking about germs. That fox-stole's got – a *curse* on it!'

Cathy looked uncertainly at the fur, which seemed quite ordinary, even to the lining having a faint wedge-shaped scorch mark where someone must have used an over-heated iron.

'It's been kind of hushed up in the family, and the only reason I know is from that secret hole I drilled under the house through our lounge-room floor,' Isobel said. 'I've picked up all sorts of interesting information listening to Mum rattling on to visitors . . . oh look, here's that scrap-book of Royal Family pictures Grace collected when she was little . . . '

'Never mind that now – tell me about Lilith.'

'I don't really like talking about it. It gives me the creeps. Listen, why don't we go out for a walk or something? We won't get many more sunny days like this . . . '

'It was *your* idea to go through Mum's box in the first place – I wanted to fix up the roof on my tree-house before winter sets in. Just tell us the rest about Lilith . . . '

'Well . . . she was supposed to be a beauty, with lovely long jet-black hair, only she was sort of peculiar. She used to wander about by the river singing at the top of her voice.'

'There's nothing peculiar about that. Heather and Vivienne do it all the time.'

'But Lilith went in for grand opera, she was totally convinced she had a voice even better than Nellie Melba's. And one day – here's where it gets interesting, some famous opera singer was staying overnight in Wilgawa on his way to somewhere else. So . . . look at this belt buckle shaped like a swan! I wonder if your mum would let me keep it . . . '

'Isobel!'

'All right, don't get impatient, I was just about to tell what happened next. Lilith rode down to town and hung about in front of the River Hotel – that's where the famous opera singer was staying. She couldn't just go in and ask to see him, ladies didn't go into pubs in those days or even talk to strange men unless they'd been introduced. So she waited and waited, and finally she had a bit of luck – he came out for a stroll and his hat blew off. Lilith ran after it and grabbed it just before it landed in the water, but she wouldn't let him have it back until he listened to her sing!'

'So what happened – did he take her away with him to join the opera?'

'What happened was he listened for about ten seconds, then told her she had the rottenest singing voice he'd ever heard in his whole life! And what's more, he told her to beetle off back home or he'd have her arrested for disturbing the peace.'

'Poor Lilith!'

'Well, actually it was what everyone else had been thinking for years. Her voice was so gruesome it used to upset the cows around Baroongal Flats, they had the lowest milk yield in the whole river district. But after that famous opera singer came right out and said it, she went back home to the farm and turned even more dotty. She stopped singing altogether, but she hardly spoke to anyone, either. She just sat around moping and staring into space, and then one evening . . . oh look, here's a nice silver earring. Maybe there might be another one and I could have them to keep . . . '

'It's not an earring, it's only the lid off a mustard cruet and you just leave Mum's souvenirs alone! Go on, tell about Lilith . . . '

'Well, one evening she was sitting droopily around saying life wasn't worth living now all her hopes of being an opera singer were dashed. But everyone was just about fed up listening to her by then, and they insisted she'd better buck up and start getting over it. They plonked down this fox-pelt in front of her and said she could make herself useful by putting in a lining . . . '

'Isobel – don't think I didn't see you sneak that fan up your sleeve!'

'Oh, did I really? How absent-minded of me, and I don't even want it, anyhow, peacock feathers are bad luck – just like Lilith's fox-fur stole. Where was I . . . oh yes, Lilith said she wouldn't live long enough to even wear that fox-stole, but they said tough luck and get cracking. I guess they were all bossing her around so much she just gave in finally, because she cut out the lining and began to sew it in. And you'll never guess what she used . . . '

'Was it this same material that's there now?'

'Yes – but remember how the man's hat blew off? Well, she'd quickly ripped out the silk lining without him noticing before she gave that hat back. Lilith wasn't Aunt Ivy's ancestor for nothing – you know how all the women in that family never throw away a single solitary thing if they think it might come in handy. So there she sat that night, stitching away muttering to herself, but no one could understand a word, because it sounded like gibberish. Then all of a sudden she yelled, 'There – now it's finished and I hope you're all happy!' and rushed outside. They were used to her acting emotional like that, but she was gone for ages so they finally started looking for her. And then . . . here's your mum's wedding veil, what a peculiar thing for her to keep! You'd think she'd have chucked it on a bonfire years ago with a whole bottle of kerosene . . . '

'*Isobel Dion!*'

'Okay, hold your horses, I was just about to tell you the rest. They had to search a long time, and it must have been a nasty shock when they found poor old Lilith. What she'd done was put some rocks in her apron pockets, then walked out into the deep part of the river and drowned herself.'

'That's . . . awful!' Cathy said, visited unnervingly by an image of long black hair fanning for an instant on moonlit water, then vanishing.

'That's why her fox-stole's been kept as a family heirloom,' Isobel explained. 'No one liked to turf it out, because it was the very last thing in the house Lilith ever touched before she died.'

'You can even see the little double stitch where she finished off the seam,' Cathy said. 'It's creepy, thinking of her just walking out into the night like that and . . . '

'There's more to come, the bit about the curse. Lilith was supposed to have placed a curse on the fox-stole while she was putting in the lining. Probably she meant it for the opera singer, because of that silk material being out of his hat, but something must have gone wrong. Everyone else has copped it instead. That fur's been handed on down through the family, but anyone who has it in their house ends up with the most shocking bad luck! Just look at the Baroongal Flats Mellings – poor old Riley dying when the tractor rolled on him, and their place getting wiped out in the big flood . . . '

'So did a lot of other people's houses up that way.'

'Yes, but that was different, they didn't have Lilith's fox-stole under their roof, did they? You only have to look at what happened to the East Wilgawa Mellings, too – Lindsay stuck in that horrible P.O.W. camp all those years, Aunty Cessie's hands crippled up with arthritis, the bridge archway falling on Uncle Trip's new car, you name it, they copped it . . . until they had the sense to pass that fur off on to someone else in the family! I guess that's how your mum must have wound up with it – Aunty Cessie eventually palmed it off on her.'

'Why didn't someone just chuck it out?'

'There's some old will and testament saying that it's not allowed to be thrown out, because of being Lilith's last relic. Everyone's got to take turns having it whether they like it or not. And just think – it's been lying there in your mum's box, maybe for years, without us knowing! Just kind of *lurking* there, with the curse all ready to ooze out . . . '

'But . . . nothing really awful ever happened to us.'

'I wouldn't say that – what about your dad's plantation failing? How about him not being able to get a job and you might even have to move again because you can't afford the rent on this house? And Viv always getting sick with her tonsils . . . there's masses of things. From what I've heard, though, the curse works much stronger if that fur-stole's actually taken out and handled. So you can thank your lucky stars I was here to warn you, Cathy. You'd better put it back and forget all about it, don't even *think* about making it up into a handbag or anything else! Listen . . . that sounds like your mum coming in the gate now, but don't say a word to her, okay? She mightn't even know about Lilith's curse, a lot of people in the family don't, and we wouldn't want to upset her.'

Mum, back from town with Heather and Vivienne and the weekend shopping, was concerned only with getting her shoes off and lying down before dinner. She left them with instructions to unpack the groceries and put them away, although the others basely left Cathy to do it all by herself. They vanished outside, but Cathy didn't mind very much – unpacking the groceries meant she could help herself to an illicit handful of dried apricots. And besides, what they were doing outside looked as though it could end up in a fight, as she saw through the kitchen window. Isobel, Heather and Vivienne were posted around the paddock using Heather's semaphore flags to send insulting messages of a personal nature to each other.

Cathy, the groceries all shelved, decided not to join them. She stayed inside and worked on the anchor-shaped patchwork cushion she was making for her lookout, even though Isobel had claimed it looked more like a drunken sailor than an anchor. The front was finished and she'd begun on the back, stitching the squares together by hand, because no one had ever been able to teach her how the sewing-machine worked. Her supply of patches was almost used up, but the scrap-bag yielded no new colour or pattern that she hadn't already used. Suddenly she thought of the brown silk lining of the fox-stole.

That ridiculous story of Isobel's about a curse – curses were only connected to exotic things like scarab medallions. Whoever heard of one being placed on a fox-stole? It was just packed away in the chest not being used, and all she needed was a very small amount of the brown silk. Perhaps it might be best not to ask Mum directly, especially now when she was having a rest . . . in fact it would be more thoughtful, really, not to bother her at all for such a paltry matter. If the lining was tacked carefully back into place after a little piece was removed, probably no one would even realise!

Cathy crept out to the cedar chest in the living-room, retrieved the stole and took it back to her room. She snipped off enough of the lining material for two patchwork squares, and using her best sewing, which Heather said was equal to everyone else's worst, repaired the damage. Then she added the squares to her cushion, thinking idly about Lilith's unfortunate fate. Maybe one day she'd write a story about Lilith and call it 'The Tragedy at Baroongal Flats' – except it might be better to think of a different place name. Baroongal Flats somehow didn't have the right ring to it . . . She grew bored with patchwork sewing, and picked up the fox-fur, still convinced that a remarkable bag could be contrived from it somehow. The mask could be folded down to make a flap, and the tail taken off and used as an overarm strap . . .

Isobel came hurtling past the window and into the house, shrieking, 'Aunty Connie! Aunty Con – there's been an accident! Vivienne's gashed her foot on a rusty old tin and she's practically bleeding to death!'

Vivienne, helped in from outside and sat down on the kitchen table, left a trail of crimson globules all over the lino. She kept her eyelids shut as tightly as valves while Mum washed out the cut with disinfectant. The sight of blood made her feel faint, which was why she'd never joined Guides with Heather and Cathy. Girl Guides were expected to learn First Aid, but Vivienne knew that anyone involved in an accident would be in a much worse state when she'd finished attending to them. Once she'd bravely tried to remove a splinter all by herself, but had squeamishly looked the other way while doing it and stabbed herself badly with the tweezers. Cathy, on the other hand, thought blood was quite a cheerful colour and watched with interest, her patchwork cushion forgotten.

'You're a silly disobedient girl, Vivienne, taking off your shoes and running around outside! I've told you and told you – people can end up with lockjaw from rusty tins and nails!' Mum said, sounding harsh because she was worried. 'That's a nasty-looking cut and it's going to need stitches. We'd better get it looked at up at the hospital, though how you're going to walk on that foot, I don't know!'

'She could sit on Heather's bike and you and me could push her up, one on each side,' Cathy said helpfully. 'Only if I'm allowed to watch while they sew her up, though. I wonder if they fold the skin over like a little hem, or just crimp the two edges together and . . . '

'Don't be so thoughtless, Cathy – you've made your sister go white as a sheet! Isobel can give me a hand pushing the bike up the hill, seeing it's about time she went home, anyway. You and Heather could give the floor a mop and get tea ready while I'm gone.'

Cathy, thinking those two jobs sounded boring, craftily left them to Heather and went to feed the chooks. They came flapping and clucking greedily about her feet as she cast handfuls of grain on the ground. Keeping a wary eye on Napoleon the rooster, who preferred human ankles, she filled the old car tyre that had been sawn in half for a water container, and then noticed a limp bundle of feathers tucked pathetically under a nearby bush.

'Heather, poor Freda's dead!' she called, but Heather, sucking a bruised finger, had no sympathy to spare for Freda, Vivienne up at the hospital, or anyone else at all.

'I jammed my knuckle in the oven door!' she howled over the veranda rail, dancing an anguished jig of pain. 'It just slammed shut all of a sudden like someone was pushing it! Pestering me about dead chooks – just dig a hole down the back and bury the damn thing!'

'I . . . can't,' Cathy said ashamedly. 'Any of the other

chooks, but not Freda! I remember her from a chick, when she pecked her way out of the egg and hopped up on my fist . . . '

'Don't be stupid – she can't just be left lying around dead. And when Mum's away, I'm in charge and you've got to do what I say!'

'If *you* bury Freda, I'll go over and fetch the cow in for the night even though it's your turn,' Cathy hedged, and before Heather could refuse, ran across the yard and into the back lane. Most of the grass in their own paddock was finished, so Mum had come to an arrangement with the brickworks manager for Mona to spend the days in the lusher grass there. Cathy opened the brickworks gate and called, but Mona didn't come ambling obediently up the slope. This evening, apparently, she'd made other plans. Cathy checked around the fence and located a fallen rail, a large manure pat sitting on the other side as triumphantly as a trophy, and hoof marks meandering up towards the sawmill and beyond. Cathy, swearing to herself, went on a long, fruitless search, then ran back and told Mum, who had just brought an impressively bandaged Vivienne home from the hospital.

'Well, we can't go out hunting for her ladyship all over the district now it's getting dark,' Mum said, harassed. 'We'll just have to hope she doesn't end up in the pound with a fine to pay to get her out . . . Goodness, Heather, is this object supposed to be shepherd's pie or an old saddle-bag?'

'It's not my fault,' Heather said huffily. 'Something went funny with the oven and it burned to a crisp in the first ten minutes.'

'Rubbish, nothing's ever gone wrong with that oven, it's always reliable as . . .*oh, sugar!*' Mum cried and stared in astonishment at the collage of broken pie-dish and charred mashed potato decorating the floor. 'Now that's very strange – that dish just slipped right through my hands as though it had a will of its own! Never mind, we'll just have to make do with leftovers on toast instead.'

They ate that in the lounge-room, listening to the wireless to compensate, but half-way through 'The Quiz Kids' a shower of soot came slithering down the chimney. It landed with a mushrooming thump, spattering the miniature oval painting Mum was copying from Hilary Melling's wedding photograph. Mum rushed to the roll-top desk to see if anything could be salvaged, but all her painstaking work – the bride's delicately stranded hair, rose-tinted cheeks and detailed bouquet – was ruined.

'I daresay it's my own fault, leaving it lying about uncovered with the paint still wet,' Mum said after a moment's silence, but her voice was heavy with regret. Vivienne, remembering that Hilary Melling's mother had promised a generous payment for the miniature, burst into tears of sympathy mingled with delayed trauma from having had stitches. Mum said briskly that she'd had quite enough excitement for one day, and declared that it was bedtime for everyone.

Cathy lay awake, with a worry that had been creeping mousily about inside her head transformed suddenly into a rampaging tiger. She'd hidden the fur with its depleted silk lining under her pillow, waiting for an opportune moment to put it back in the cedar chest without being caught. Slowly, she pulled it out and looked at it. The fox's amber eyes regarded her glassily in the moonlight, like . . . like eyes gazing blindly up through the depths of river water! Maybe . . . maybe it should have been left safely rolled up in the chest, and she shouldn't even have touched it in the first place! All these troubles that had happened in one evening . . . Isobel had warned her about Lilith's curse, but she'd chosen to take no notice.

And now she vaguely remembered other misfortunes that had come upon various relatives – not just the East Wilgawa and the Baroongal Flats ones, either! Hadn't there been a cousin twice-removed whose hair had mysteriously started falling out when she was still in her twenties? Perhaps *she'd* handled Lilith's fox-stole at some stage! And there was Isobel's mother's sister, the one Dad called Diamond Lulu, who'd run off with someone else's husband and no one talked about her any more. Also an Edward Melling struck by lightning, and Aunt Elsie where Grace was staying down in the city – Aunt Elsie had recently had a lot of trouble with varicose veins . . .

Things like that could happen to *her* family now that the fox-fur was in their custody and she'd so rashly taken a piece of the lining for patchwork! In fact, she'd probably set that curse well and truly in action again, for the awful things had started to happen already! Cathy counted them feverishly in her mind – Vivienne's cut foot, the dead hen (for even though Freda had most likely died from old age, it seemed an odd coincidence), Heather squashing her finger in the oven door, Mona straying off, Mum dropping the inexplicably burnt shepherd's pie, the fall of soot ruining the little oil painting! All those calamities were the legacy of Lilith's curse – and even worse things could happen . . .

They could perhaps lose this house, even though Dad was searching valiantly for work all over the district. Maybe Lilith would force them to live in a humpy like poor old Mr Wetherell from Conifer Crossing! Or . . . something could happen to prevent Grace's intended visit home. Mum was looking forward to that so much it was positively heart-rending, and they all knew she was secretly hoping that Grace would decide to take a job in Wilgawa and not go back to the city at all. But Lilith would soon fix that, she might even arrange for the train Grace was travelling on to . . .

A great crash set the beaded fringe of the hall lamp tinkling like a chime of bells. Cathy, appalled, leaped out of bed and rushed up the hall to Mum's room, but Mum was on the floor with the brass bed collapsed beneath her, and in no position to offer comfort to anyone. The base of the bed had somehow worked loose from the sockets, but Cathy, trembling with scared guilt, knew it was no accident.

'I'm all right, it's only my dignity's been hurt,' Mum said, picking herself up. 'You can just go and tell that tactless Heather and Vivienne to stop carrying on about earthquakes, and while you're about it, bring me the hammer so I can dong this old bed back together again.'

'I don't think you'd better, you'll . . . you'll only miss and do yourself an injury! Lilith's out to get us . . . ' Cathy said, and began gabbling incoherently about opera singers, fox-stoles and curses from watery graves.

'Lilith – who on earth is Lilith?' Mum demanded in bewilderment, peering at the fur thrust waveringly under her nose. 'I can scarcely take in one word you're saying, Cathy! Your dad never even *had* an Aunt Lilith as far as I know. And as for this fox-scarf, you're a naughty girl helping yourself to bits of the lining without even asking! Even if it *is* just an old thing Mrs O'Keefe gave me a few weeks ago because she thought it was a shame to throw out . . . Anyhow, I've already promised it to Isobel.'

'*Isobel*?'

'Well, I suppose this is what she was carrying on about when she helped me take Viv up to the hospital. She kept pestering me about some old fox-fur in my box, asking if she could have it to keep next time she dropped in. I don't for the life of me know why she'd possibly want it, but she did say something about making herself a handbag.'

# *An Act of Luminous Goodness*

'Meet you back here at five-thirty on the dot,' Heather said when they were through the turnstile. 'And if you spend all your money in the first ten minutes, just don't come tagging after me trying to cadge, because you won't get a single penny! Don't either of you *dare* tag after me, anyway – I've arranged to meet a . . . someone I know from school.'

Vivienne had no intention of wasting her carefully hoarded money in the first ten minutes. Eight shillings and sixpence in small change jingled delightfully in her purse, each coin representing thrift and labour. Cathy had charged off, as she did every year, towards the amusement rides, but Vivienne wasn't planning to have even one turn on the merry-go-round. Ever since the age of five, she'd secretly yearned to buy a doll-on-a-stick at the Show. Cathy always jeered about them and said they looked like torsos drowning in plates of chopped-up jelly, but she didn't care what Cathy thought. This year she was going to spend all her money on one of those dolls! It was really just a matter of self-discipline, of walking firmly past fairy-floss stalls, hoopla booths and merry-go-rounds.

She passed the Octopus, thinking how aptly named it was with those long tentacles that whisked people, screaming, up into the sky above the tent tops. It was hard to understand why anyone would want to pay to be terrified, but Cathy, who understood very well, had already joyously exchanged sixpence for a ticket. Vivienne left her to it and began a methodical search for dolls-on-sticks, heroically averting her eyes from such goodies as crisp waffles filled with cream, or the marvellous rainbow ice-creams that were obtainable only at the Show once a year. Heather, who'd found her way to the miniature rifle-range, was eating one of those ice-creams. She was also screeching idiotically at each rifle shot, and Vivienne glanced at her in surprise. Heather wasn't in the least frightened of guns, having gone rabbiting quite often with Uncle Trip, but now for some reason she was pretending to be startled by the noise. That big gawky boy firing at the target of painted ducks must think she was a pest, and it was a wonder he didn't turn around and tell her to shut up!

Vivienne walked on, stopping to inspect booths that sold dolls-on-sticks, but also making a detour into the exhibits hall to see Aunt Ivy's prize-winning decorated cake. Aunt Ivy would be deeply offended if none of them could describe it on her next visit. Because of the crowd inside the hall, a glimpse of that cake also meant a slow forced circuit of the other exhibits all the way around to the other door. She passed the trestle tables of bottled fruits, admiring their luscious symmetry, but made faintly uneasy by the sheer number of jars. It was as though people secretly believed that the annual bounty should be cached in case another summer never came.

Once outside, she resumed her important search. The

dolls-on-sticks varied in quality and price from stall to stall, but she meant to examine every single one, realising how difficult it was going to be to make a final choice. They were all gorgeous with their bright eyes and little dimpled hands, their net skirts sprinkled with silver or gold. Cathy always said that as well as looking like torsos in plates of jelly, they'd make very good blowfly swatters, but her opinion didn't count. The only doll she'd ever shown any interest in was one she'd once made from a melted candle, sticking pins in it to get revenge on Isobel. Besides, Cathy's main purpose in coming to the Show every year was to ride on dangerous things like the Octopus and to sneak into the sideshows without paying.

Vivienne walked up an alley between two lines of side-shows, but stumbled over a pair of legs on the ground. She kicked at them indignantly, recognising the socks, and Cathy scrambled up from where she'd been endeavouring to peer under a tent.

'Oh, I wish I hadn't spent all my money already!' Cathy mourned. 'The Incredible Half-Man's in this tent, but you can't see a thing from here. They've got it blocked off with screens. I reckon he's probably split down the middle with only one nostril and one eye and an arm and a leg all on the same side. He'd have to get around by hopping, though it must be pretty tiring . . . how about lending us sixpence to get in?'

'Nothing doing,' Vivienne said decisively.

'Once you're in there you can chat to him, it says so on the notice. They should only charge half price to get in, really. Wow, I've never talked to anyone with only half a mouth before, let alone seen one!'

'Don't be so horrible, Cathy – you *can't* want to gawk

at someone like that! The poor thing – it must be awful having to travel round with the Show and have people stare at you.'

'Only half of you, and no one's forcing him to, anyway. He'd be used to it, and he probably earns a fortune, though it must be kind of hard to chat to people with only half a tongue. I wonder what he really looks like . . . Oh, come on, Viv, lend us some dough!'

'No I won't, and you ought to be ashamed of yourself acting like all those other stickybeak people! Just *look* at them, falling over each other to get inside!' Vivienne said, frowning righteously at the people in the queue with their nasty, morbid curiosity.

'If you shout us in, I'll pay you back soon – honest,' Cathy wheedled.

'Go away. I need all my money for something else.'

'Right then, you selfish little hog, just wait till you want something off *me*!' Cathy said and stormed off in the direction of the Ferris wheel.

Vivienne stood fingering the clasp of her purse, reading the notice above the tent entrance. There could be some truth in what Cathy had said, she thought absently – the Half-Man might be making a fortune, and perhaps really didn't mind being stared at. He could even feel quite flattered because so many people wanted to meet him. In fact, if you *didn't* go in, his feelings might be hurt, he could even think you were insulting him! And another thing . . . if someone were to go in there and just take one quick look then come right out again, it wouldn't really count as stickybeaking . . .

Sixpence to get in . . . that would mean less to spend on a doll, but she'd still have her untouched eight shillings.

She sacrificed the sixpence for a ticket and went inside the tent. At first she could see nothing but a wall of backs, but managed to burrow through to a small space at the end of a rope barrier. Someone trod massively on her toe but didn't apologise, and she realised suddenly that no one was talking, not even in whispers. The crowd was self-consciously silent, staring, and pretending not to, across the rope at the Half-Man. Vivienne stared, too, at an ordinary middle-aged face with greying hair slicked back with brilliantine, at a clean white shirt, a tie fastened with a horseshoe tie-pin, then . . . nothing. The Half-Man was balanced on the palms of his hands, using them as feet, for his truncated body ended where his hips should have begun. He walked on his hands to and fro about the raised platform, then hoisted himself into a chair – one that looked more like a bizarre cradle. A guitar lay beside it. He strummed a few popular songs, then smiled politely at everyone and said he would be happy to answer any questions.

Nobody asked any. The silence was gluey with embarrassment.

'Well then – my name's Ralph Esmond and I'm fifty-three years old. I was born like this, it wasn't because of an accident,' the Half-Man said, helping them patiently along as though they were bashful children in a class-room. 'I've always tried to overcome my great handicap as best I could . . .'

Vivienne, making herself as unobtrusive as possible, stepped backwards, no longer wanting to look. There was something devastating about the collective embarrassment within the tent, the nervously smothered titters, the man's resigned courtesy. Something deplorable . . .

'I can get about, after a fashion,' the gentle, tired voice

recited mechanically, as though innumerable recitations had been delivered to countless tent audiences, year after year. 'My health is quite good. I have normal organs . . . '

Vivienne, diminished by private shame, crept along behind the row of backs and went out into the clattering brightness of the showground, hurrying away from the side-show tents. In her resumed search for a doll-on-a-stick she passed Heather, who didn't even notice. Heather was tossing quoits at tawdry prizes on a hoopla stand. She was still acting unaccountably silly, pretending that she couldn't throw very well, even though she was in the high school volleyball team. And there was another thing – since flouncing off so mysteriously at the turnstile entrance, she'd somehow acquired and applied bright red lipstick! Vivienne eyed the lipstick with disapproval, also noticing that the same boy who'd been at the rifle-range was now loitering around the hoopla stall. He suddenly snatched one of Heather's quoits and dodged away with it. Heather chased after him, giggling, and they scuffled together in a ridiculous dance amongst the tent-pegs and ropes.

Vivienne walked on, not even bothering to look at the hoopla prizes. The only objects worth winning on that stall were the brass statuettes depicting Diana, goddess of the hunt, but she knew from past experience that they were displayed only as bait. Those statuettes were all placed at cunning, impossible angles where no quoits could land. She gripped her purse and marched staunchly by, taking a short cut through the livestock section. Eleanor Grantby's grandfather was in there and raised his hat to her, making her feel wonderfully grown-up. He asked how Grace was faring in the city, for Eleanor and Grace had been friends at school, then boasted at some length about his pigs. Vivienne admired the pigs and finally escaped, making a detour through the refreshment shed.

She cast a hungry eye at the sausage-rolls and scones, but managed to get herself and her unopened purse safely away. There were more dolls-on-sticks in the booths by the far fence. She hurried down a path between two rows of parked cars, but someone was blocking the exit at the far end. Phyllis Gathin . . . Vivienne's pace slowed instinctively and almost stopped altogether, for no one could possibly be seen talking to Phyllis Gathin! Phyllis hadn't gone on to high school, but had been kept down in sixth class because of poor work. She also had an embarrassing tendency to smile at Vivienne on the strength of having been in the same class-room as Cathy last year. Her diffident, fragile smile was in some strange way as compelling as a weapon, making you feel cruel if you didn't respond, no matter how much you didn't wish to.

Phyllis wasn't alone, she was minding one of her grubby little sisters. In one hand she carried a red bantam chook with its feet tied and in the other a string bag loaded with bottled cordial and bananas that had reached the soft brownish stage. *Nobody*, Vivienne thought with scathing pity, brought along food and drink from home to eat at the Show, it just wasn't done! And everyone, no matter how poor, dressed up in their best outfits to come to the Easter Show – some people even bought new clothes specially for the occasion. But Phyllis Gathin and her sister were dressed as they always were, in abominable faded garments that were . . . background-coloured, Vivienne thought, foraging in her mind for the right word, background-coloured, just like Phyllis Gathin's humble, camouflaged personality. She turned to duck out of sight between two parked cars, but the Gathins had already seen her.

They stepped aside automatically, allowing her right of way, flattening themselves against the side of a van as though that was expected of them, too. Phyllis smiled at her wistfully and Vivienne made the mistake of saying, 'Oh . . . hello, you look as though you've got your hands full . . . '

Phyllis, beaming because someone had actually spoken to her, began a long, barely audible saga about bringing young Greta to the Show, how they'd found threepence on the ground, won the bantam hen in a lucky number draw, seen the mechanical cow in the exhibits hall with stuff that looked like real milk pinging out into a little bucket, watched the big draught-horses in the ring . . .

'Tell her about . . . ' little Greta Gathin whispered every time Phyllis stopped for breath, and Vivienne, trapped by a nature that wouldn't allow her to be openly mean to anyone, even Gathins, shuffled from foot to foot with concealed impatience.

They'd seen all the lovely iced cakes in the hall, watched the men in the wood-chopping competition, Greta had found a runaway balloon, but then it blew away and someone trod on it . . . The little girl's eyes fogged with that recent sorrow, and Vivienne said quickly, 'I've got to rush, got to meet my sisters soon . . . ' She fled away into the crowd, deliberately altering course several times in case Phyllis had it in mind to follow, and paused for breath by an enormous merry-go-round, new to the Show this year. It was just as overwhelming as everyone at school had claimed, with free-flying horses that soared and swung wide, so that the riders were almost parallel to the ground.

Cathy was there, hanging over the rail, her face tense with longing. 'Oh quick, Viv – lend us sixpence!' she pleaded, like a famished beggar.

'I already said no! You shouldn't have spent all your money on those other rides soon as we got here . . . '

'I *had* to go on the Octopus!' Cathy said indignantly. 'That's the first thing I ever do when we get to the Show. Then the Ferris wheel . . . guess what – it broke down while I was on it and my seat got stuck for ages right up the top!'

Vivienne clutched her stomach, not wanting to hear. She didn't really like watching the huge new carousel with its whirling horses, either.

'Lucky I had a meat pie and a waffle to eat while I was up on the Ferris wheel,' Cathy said. 'And I didn't spend all my money on rides, either – I went in the House of Horrors, too. They've got that gorilla jumping out at you on the way in, but it's just someone dressed up. Heather was in there – you should have heard her holler about the gorilla! Stupid dill, she even grabbed this boy's hand and hung on to him, dunno what *he* must have thought! She went in the House of Horrors last year and it was the same gorilla, only she never screamed then. Pleeeease, Viv, lend us some money for a go on the merry-go-round!'

Vivienne stubbornly shook her head.

'If you don't . . . I'll *steal* a ride!' Cathy threatened.

'Cathy, you're not to – it's dangerous! I'll tell Mum on you . . . '

'Stewart Thurlow's been pinching rides all afternoon, so's Danny O'Keefe, I've been watching them. O'Keefe reckoned I couldn't do it in a frothy-mouthed fit, but there's nothing to it, really. You just wait till the man's gone round and collected everyone's tickets, then . . . '

Vivienne grabbed at her in alarm, but Cathy was already over the rail and scampering along beside the moving carousel. She leaped high, grabbed the mane of a vacant horse, and swung herself up. The ticket-collector yelled and shook a fist, but Cathy stuck out a length of tongue and settled back to enjoy the stolen ride. Vivienne, deeply ashamed of being related to her at that moment, hurried away. She went to a stall she'd noticed earlier by the turnstiles, one that stocked a large range of dolls-on-sticks. She inspected them intently, and at last, as though it had been waiting there trustingly for her all through the afternoon, found her heart's desire. Everything about the doll was perfect, its little feathery cap, the circular golden skirt with scarlet spangles, the elegant curve of the bamboo stick decorated with a shining bow . . .

'Oooh – that's *lovely*! Are you really gonna buy it, Viv?' a self-effacing voice murmured in her ear.

Vivienne, irked at being accosted by Phyllis Gathin yet again, feigned deafness and began to count out her precious coins.

'This the one you want?' the stall-holder asked. 'But you've only given me eight bob – the ones with the gilt skirts cost eight and six.'

Vivienne stared at her, uncomprehending. That doll was *hers*! She'd searched for it all afternoon, denying herself the other wonders of the Show, even the melting magic of fairy-floss, that fleeting whisper of sweetness obtainable only once a year! Her beautiful doll-on-a-stick, exactly the right one – she could see herself bearing it proudly home and attaching it to her bedpost where it would remain for ever and ever . . .

'But . . . it was right here with all those others marked

eight shillings!' If only she hadn't bought that ticket to see the Half-Man, she'd have enough money! It was like a judgement for snooping into other people's misfortunes . . . 'Eight shillings is all I've got!'

'Well, I'm sorry, love, but it must have got in with those cheaper ones by mistake. How about that nice purple doll instead? You've got enough to buy that – or the little pink fluffy one down the end.'

'But I wanted . . . I picked out . . . ' Vivienne stammered, her voice cracking with bereavement. Wordlessly, she made to put the gold doll back on the stand, but Phyllis Gathin, the most unlikely defender in the world, suddenly took it from her and held it out to the woman.

'Maybe it's been bunged in with those cheap ones on purpose – because of the tear in the little frock,' Phyllis Gathin said. She inserted first one finger, then another, through a small split in the skirt, which Vivienne hadn't even noticed, and waggled them about.

'So what?' the woman said disagreeably. 'People come by and prod and poke at things all day long – and it's only on the seam really, that hole. Just needs a couple of stitches . . . '

'All split open it is,' Phyllis said, softly and reasonably. 'Not nearly as good as them other eight-and-six ones. *They* don't have big gappy holes in the skirts.'

Vivienne glanced at her in stupefaction, for Phyllis Gathin never argued with anyone, always flattened herself against walls to concede everyone else right-of-way . . .

'It's been sitting here in this eight-bob stand all day, first thing I spotted when we come in through the gate. They must of marked down that gold doll-on-a-stick because of the dirty big hole in the frock, I remember thinking . . . '

Phyllis Gathin murmured to no one in particular. Her eyes were fastened meekly upon the ground, but it seemed as though she could perhaps stand there all evening discussing the tiny defect in the gold fabric.

'Well . . . I suppose she can have it for the same price as those cheaper ones,' the woman said grudgingly at last.

Vivienne, exulting, carried the doll away to the bench by the turnstile and sat down to wait for Heather and Cathy. The tempo of the Show was slowing a little in the lull between afternoon and evening sessions, some of the stalls closing. She fastened the buttons on her cardigan, for it was growing cold as the sun dipped down behind the big Norfolk Pines at the edge of the grounds. People were starting to leave now, going home for tea. She felt ravenously hungry, but what did it matter that she hadn't had a bite to eat since leaving home? Or that she hadn't tried her luck on the hoopla stall, had her fortune told or paid for her profile to be snipped expertly in black paper and framed? All those things shrivelled to complete unimportance beside the reality of owning such a beautiful doll-on-a-stick! Mellowed by possession, she didn't mind very much that the Gathins had trailed after her to the bench and that Phyllis's sister was crowding up close to look.

'She's that crazy about dolls, but she won't touch, she never touches nothin,' Phyllis said.

The intensity of the little girl's admiration was somehow pleasing. Vivienne twirled the stick, making the doll waltz, and Greta Gathin smiled. It was the first time she'd smiled all afternoon, Vivienne thought idly, but if you were a Gathin, you undoubtedly didn't have much to smile about. She peered over the child's head, looking out for Heather and Cathy, hoping they wouldn't be much longer. Time to go home now, time to take her wonderful new treasure home . . .

'. . . could be Shirley,' Phyllis Gathin was whispering to her little sister. 'Maggie, maybe – or Viv might pick out Greta, just the same as your name.'

Greta – she certainly wouldn't be choosing a common name like that for her lovely doll-on-a-stick, Vivienne thought, insulted, wishing that Phyllis Gathin's sister would stop breathing all over it. Although, for a tiny kid not even at school yet, Greta was being remarkably restrained, keeping her hands clasped behind her back and just gazing with wide brown eyes . . .

'I guess . . . I guess she could hold it for a minute,' Vivienne said impulsively. 'Only by the stick part, though, and just till the others come.'

Little Greta Gathin couldn't quite believe such fortune. Her hands had to be coaxed around the stick, but when she realised she was actually holding the doll, her face seemed to become illuminated. Vivienne felt warmly benign for having caused that glow. People were so nasty to the Gathins. Nobody ever made room for poor Phyllis in the school shelter-shed when it rained, for instance. And when lemonade was served at the last break-up picnic, she hadn't brought a cup as you were supposed to. Nobody had lent theirs, either, because they didn't want to drink from the same one, so she'd missed out on the lemonade. Everyone gossiped about Mrs Gathin, too, how she couldn't even manage to look after all the children she had, let alone add to their number year by year . . .

'Pretty . . . oooh, pretty!' Greta Gathin whispered to herself. She jiggled the stick so that the doll appeared to bow in all its splendour.

Vivienne smiled with absent-minded indulgence. For suddenly she was watching a gracious vision of herself entering the doorway of a hovel – somewhat like the Gathins' house in Greenforest Lane. The hovel was crowded with pathetic raggedy children, and in one corner was a rough bed covered by hessian sacks instead of blankets. A pale gaunt woman lay under the sacks, coughing in great, wracking feverish spasms. Vivienne saw herself, quite clearly, bringing order to the miserable chaos. She bathed the woman's forehead, chopped wood for a fire, made nourishing broth and fed it to all the starving waifs. On her hands and knees she scrubbed the floor, then arranged wildflowers in a jam jar on the window ledge. Cleanliness and comfort flowed from her generous toiling hands like sunshine. The wretched hovel was transformed, the children became brown-eyed beauties as she removed layers of grime from their poor little faces and dressed them in freshly laundered clothes. She opened a suitcase she'd brought with her and gave them each a present – gave away all her own belongings, the handkerchiefs Aunt Ivy had sent last birthday, her treasured books and the new shoes Mum had bought her for Christmas. Small innocent hands clung to hers in gratitude, the woman beckoned her to the bedside and murmured in a frail voice, 'Six long weeks I've been lying here and not one soul came to help – they were all too scared they'd pick up the fever. But you came, and there's only one word to describe you, Vivienne Melling – you're a *saint*!'

The poignant beauty of the vision made Vivienne blink with emotion. She would, of course, contract that fever, for she wasn't strong. Delicate, Mum called her, with all those painfully infected throats and sore ears she kept getting, and Doctor Caulfield saying her tonsils would have to come out eventually. In fact, she'd probably *die* from that fever – but they'd have a magnificent funeral for her, the whole population of Wilgawa lining the streets as the hearse passed by. For the story would soon spread, how she'd selflessly given her life to help people less fortunate. There might even be some kind of monument erected in her honour, her name emblazoned in gold letters on a block of granite . . .

'Vivienne, hurry up, we're going home now,' Heather called from the turnstile.

'Give the doll back, Greta,' Phyllis said.

Vivienne, still enraptured from her vision, put out a hand for the doll, and saw something begin to glitter in the little girl's eyes. The glitter took substance, traced two slow rolling paths down grimy cheeks. Vivienne's hand wavered.

'Greta!' Phyllis scolded, forcibly removing small fingers. 'Leggo – or I'll knock you clear into the middle of next week!'

The little girl clung to the stick, whimpering quietly. She put her head back and keened her anguish into the sky, a muted sound, scarcely louder than the hunger of fledglings in a nest.

'Gee, I dunno – she's never done nothin like this before,' Phyllis Gathin said with helpless shame. 'Never a boo out of her half the time . . . give that doll right back, Greta, or I'll fetch you such a wallop!'

'It's . . . it's all right. She can . . . she can keep it,' Vivienne said, and whirled buoyantly away through the turnstile as though she had wings on her shoes. She floated up the hill after Heather and Cathy, awed by the sacrifice she'd just made. Soon she would mention it casually to the others, she thought, but for the moment hugged it to herself. It wasn't every day you discovered such heights of luminous goodness within your soul, a nobility you hadn't even realised you possessed!

The other two were also in high spirits. Cathy was hopping jauntily along with one foot in the gutter and the other on the kerb, crowing to herself. '*Three* times I managed to jump up on that new merry-go-round and get a free ride!' she boasted. 'You should have seen me! Once on the grey dapple horse, then the white one with the red reins, then the black prancy one! Stewart Thurlow was watching – so was Danny O'Keefe! I reckon just about *everyone* saw me do it . . . That was the best time I've ever had at any Show I've ever been to!'

Cathy is just so childish for her age, Vivienne thought loftily. What she did counts for nothing, all it amounts to is being good at jumping! She's going to feel so greedy and ashamed when I tell her what I did! Heather, too, scoffing rainbow ice-creams and spending her money on the House of Horrors and all those other things . . .

'I had a super time, too, it's been the best Show ever!' Heather carolled, using her handkerchief to delete traces of lipstick before Mum could see. She carried, with great tenderness, a brass statuette of Diana, goddess of the hunt, and kept stopping to polish bits of it with her sleeve.

No one had ever been known to win one of those prizes at the hoopla stall before, Vivienne thought enviously. Perhaps somebody else had actually done the winning and then given the statuette to Heather, the elation in her face certainly hinted at that. The joyful elation of someone who'd been given a marvellous, unexpected gift, just like Phyllis Gathin's little sister . . .

Vivienne suddenly began to walk less quickly, dragging her feet as they turned the corner into the river road. She was thinking about her beautiful doll-on-a-stick. What a wonderfully charitable thing she'd done, how saintly she'd been! Phyllis Gathin's sister would be walking home to her terrible house right now, her drab life brightened by some-one else's unselfishness . . .

Vivienne clenched her own hand – her empty hand, and began to sniffle quietly to herself.

'A certain person's blubbing about something, not mentioning any names,' Cathy said, looking back with mild interest. Heather turned around and asked what was wrong, then came all the way back down the slope, for the sniffles had become a torrent of noisy scalding tears.

'Whatever's the matter?' Heather asked anxiously as Vivienne wailed and wept, thinking of her doll-on-a-stick.

'Viv, what on earth's the matter?'

Her wonderful doll-on-a-stick, being carried home by that . . . that horrible, dirty, ugly, thieving little pig of a Gathin child!

'Have you got a stomach ache? Did you eat too much fairy-floss at the Show? Say something, for goodness' sake!' Heather demanded, but Vivienne didn't say anything, not knowing how to explain that saintliness wasn't all it was cracked up to be.

## ♂ Treasure Hunt

Cathy perched on a set of old parallel bars behind the bicycle shed, feeling miserably neglected by her best friend. Barbara had practically ignored her ever since Gillian Ogden had been transferred from 1C to 1B a fortnight ago. This morning in Cookery they'd paired off at one work-table, palming Cathy casually on to Marjorie Powell, who'd made her take the measuring jug with the indecipherable markings. Her scones had come out looking like buttons. Normally that wouldn't have bothered her in the slightest, but Gillian and Barbara's combined effort had produced scones that practically floated off the baking tray. The afternoon was turning out badly, too, because she'd worn sandshoes to school, even though it wasn't a sports afternoon. Her proper school shoes, stuffed full of newspapers, were drying out at home, having been temporarily lost overboard while she was fooling about with her home-made canoe in the river. A teacher supervising the tuckshop queue had noticed and given her a hundred lines. There'd been a time when Barbara Sylvester would have cheerfully done half those lines for her, but now she was too busy fawning over that Gillian!

'It was an ice-cream cake with blue candles and my name in little blue rosebuds,' Gillian was saying. 'And if we'd been hanging round together then, Barb, I'd have invited *you* instead of that stuck-up Jeanette Everett and her crowd. But you can definitely come to my next birthday party . . . '

Cathy cleared her throat loudly, but Gillian didn't even turn around. She was showing Barbara the wonderful watch with its gold safety-chain she'd got for her birthday.

'*Everyone* gets watches when they turn twelve,' Cathy said aggressively. 'I could have picked a watch, too, but I didn't even want one. I'm getting something a whole lot more exciting. As it so happens I*'m* having a birthday party tomorrow.'

'But your birthday was last week, wasn't it?' Barbara said.

'So what? No rule says you have to have the party on the exact same day. Anyhow, I put it off because the weather was so bad.'

'You never even mentioned you were having a party,' Barbara said. 'You didn't last year – come to think of it, you've never *ever* had one before.'

'This time's different. I don't reckon the years before you turn twelve amount to all that much, so it's better to save up and have one big glittery party in one go.'

'I had balloons dusted all over with glitter,' Gillian said. 'Blue and white to match the cake decorations.'

Cathy glared at her, wishing that people who owned magnificent gold watches with safety-chains and stole other people's best friends had never shown a sudden aptitude and been moved up to 1B. 'Balloons are babyish,' she said. 'You might as well play games like Drop the Hanky. I'm planning to . . . to hire the ferry tomorrow and hold my birthday party out in the middle of the river! I bet no one's ever thought of doing that before.'

Gillian and Barbara finally gave her their full attention, and Cathy, satisfied, rolled backwards on the parallel bars to dangle by her knees.

'If the party's on tomorrow, how come you haven't handed out any invitations yet?' Barbara asked.

'I sent them out by post,' Cathy lied, for nothing at all was happening tomorrow. Her birthday, partyless, had come and gone the previous Saturday, accompanied by disappointing presents – a pocket dictionary from Grace, a card from Heather and Vivienne with a promise of chocolates that hadn't eventuated yet, a much-less-than-expected postal note sent by her godmother, and a silly poodle brooch from Isobel with a safety-pin clasp instead of a proper one. Her official birthday present, the raincoat on lay-by at Osborne's, must languish there until Mum was less woefully short of money. In fact, it had been very much like all her other birthdays, not even remotely in the same category as ice-cream cakes decorated with blue rosebuds and glittery balloons.

'Can Gillian and me come?' Barbara asked.

'You'll just have to wait and see if the postie brings you anything in the mail,' Cathy said archly, confident of being able to think of some plausible reason on Monday to explain why no invitations had arrived.

She certainly had plenty of time for thinking next day, being alone with nothing much to do. Heather was away on a Guide hike, and Vivienne, miserably recovering from yet another bout of tonsillitis, had been taken by Mum as a treat to visit Aunt Cessie over the river. Dad was renovating some piece of old junk out in the shed. He, too, had time on his hands, for the racetrack caretaker job he'd applied for had gone to someone else. When she offered to help with whatever he was doing in the shed, he told her ungratefully to expect a thick ear if she came out there bothering him. He'd been irritable and troubled lately, which was probably why, Cathy decided shrewdly, Mum had chosen to go out for the day.

She lazed about on the front steps, trying to think of something interesting to do. There was always Isobel's house, but Isobel drove everyone mad with hideous renditions of 'Lady of Spain' ever since taking up the accordion. She could go up the road to the O'Keefes', and run races with them, but they weren't very good sports. When they lost they'd bash you up, and if they won they tended to jump about triumphantly and yell, 'Yah – who's an old puffed-out granny at running, then?' There was always the river, but that was depressing now that her lovely galvanised-iron canoe was somewhere in the middle filling up with silt. All the back-breaking hours spent hammering that sheet of iron into shape and plugging the holes and cracks . . . she'd never have the heart to make another one! And the excursions she'd planned – upriver as far as the little island and all the way down again to the ferry-crossing! She could have paddled past the Sylvesters' backyard and not even offered Barbara a ride now she'd deserted her best friend and taken up with Gillian Ogden instead. The unspeakable treachery of that snake in the grass Barbara Sylvester . . .

. . . who was strolling down the hospital hill this very minute dressed to the nines, accompanied by Gillian Ogden carrying a package wrapped unmistakably in birthday present paper! Cathy looked away and counted slowly to fifty, concentrating on a knee patch in the old pedal-pushers she'd inherited from Heather. She hoped that the other thing was just a mirage, like the heat haze that shimmered above road surfaces in summer, but when she finished counting, they were both walking in through the front gate.

'Hi, Cathy – happy birthday!' Barbara said. 'Those invitations you posted didn't come in this morning's mail, but we knew you'd be really disappointed if we didn't turn up. Gosh, I hope we aren't too early . . . you haven't even had time to get changed yet!'

Cathy remembered with horror that as well as the awful old pedal-pushers, she'd grabbed a checked shirt straight off the clothesline without bothering to iron it. 'It's . . . it's sensible to wear old clothes when you're getting everything ready for a party,' she said quickly.

'You *did* mean I was invited, too, didn't you?' Gillian asked. 'Barbie said I would be, even though I only just moved into 1B. She was so positive about it we went downtown and bought this birthday present together – here, it's from the two of us.'

Cathy removed the wrapping and stared blankly at the *Girl's Crystal Annual* within. At any other time she would have been delighted, but now had no room in her mind except for embarrassment. Barbara and Gillian, she knew, were exchanging covert glances, obviously wondering why she wasn't asking them in.

'Er . . . parties usually start at three, don't they?' Barbara asked uncomfortably. 'Haven't any of the others turned up yet? Oooh, Cathy, supposing they didn't get *their* invitations in the post, either! The same thing happened to my sister Belle once – she got asked to this engagement party and didn't even know it was on because the card went missing in the mail!'

'I know – maybe they think we're all supposed to meet at the ferry!' Gillian said brightly.

'Ferry?' Cathy echoed.

'Well, if you mentioned in the invitation about having afternoon tea there, they might think that. Oh, I'm really looking forward to that part, I've never actually ever been on a boat before. And your special birthday present you're getting, can we . . . '

'Wait . . . wait here, I'll be back in a minute!' Cathy babbled. She spun around the side of the house, dashed across the paddock and flung herself, wailing, at Dad.

'Told you not to come pestering me when I'm in the middle of working,' he said, pushing her bad-temperedly out of the shed. 'What's all the blubbing about, anyhow? If you went for a sixer off that roof again, it's your own fault shinning up there in the first place.'

'I never! Oh, Dad . . . '

'Be a man, there's a good girl, you know I can't stand tears! I never bloody know how to deal with sooking . . . can't you save it up for when your mum gets home?'

Cathy shook her head desperately. 'You'd be blubbing, too, if something as awful as this happened to you! I sort of . . . let on to these girls at school I was having a birthday party and now they've turned up on our doorstep! There's only half a date-loaf left in the kitchen and no proper milk, only a tin of condensed, so I can't even offer them afternoon tea! And that's not all of it, either, I said . . . said I'd be hiring the ferry and holding my party out in the middle of the river!'

'Serves you right, telling big fat whoppers like that!'

Dad scolded, handing her a scrap of painty rag to dab her eyes with. 'Though, mind you, you could always rig up that old army tent in the paddock and let on it's a marquee. And make some damper with a few candles stuck in the top . . . '

'It's not funny!' Cathy cried indignantly. 'I'll never hear the end of it from that Barbara Sylvester – she'll blab it around to everyone else at school! Oh, what am I going to *do*? They're out there on the front path right now, whispering to each other . . . '

'You can still bung on a party, no worries,' Dad said. 'If the tucker's not flash, the entertainment can make up for it. Let's see now . . . ' He licked a stub of carpenter's pencil and wrote something on the back of a receipt from the Hay and Corn Store, elbowing Cathy smartly out of the way when she tried to pry. Then he tore the paper into three sections, put them in an old envelope and headed for the front yard. Cathy followed dismally, not convinced that anything jotted on three slips of paper could remedy the situation. And Dad, she thought with sudden embarrassment, didn't look as respectable as Mr Sylvester or Gillian Ogden's father. For a start, there were his clothes – worn corduroy breeches, leather leggings, and the terrible old sweater Mum kept putting in the rag bag and he kept fishing out. There was his limp, too, and although he'd got that from being in the Light Horse Brigade, which was undoubtedly glamorous, his rolling walk looked a bit odd. It didn't help, either, that he always tried to disguise the limp by charging bravely about like a troop of cavalry. It unnerved people, that rushing walk, specially when accompanied by a stare from piercing blue eyes under shaggy eyebrows.

'G'day there, young ladies,' Dad said affably to Gillian

and Barbara. 'It's not just anyone who's been invited along today, so count yourselves lucky. Specially as there's going to be a treasure hunt.'

'Oh . . . that sounds fun, Mr Melling,' Barbara said politely.

Dad looked at her and she wilted, edging uneasily closer to Gillian Ogden.

'Who said anything about fun?' he demanded. 'I can tell you one thing straight off – you should've worn sensible duds like young Cathy here, not those frippery articles all over tucks and ribbons. Now, I've put the treasure hunt instructions in this envelope, all numbered in the right order, one, two, three.'

'Only three?' Gillian said. 'With treasure hunts you usually have lots. At *my* birthday party we hid dozens of little notes all over the house saying things like, "Look under the lace runner on the dressing-table" . . . '

'You want to play a pappy cubby-house game like that, you should have brought along a bib and rattle,' Dad said crushingly. 'Lace runners on dressing-tables, my eye! This one's different, and maybe you'll come through it all right – or then again maybe you won't. You'll find out soon enough. Get yourselves down to Slidemaster Street and open that first bit of paper – right in front of the police station, but don't expect me to come down there and bail any of you out if . . . never mind. *Danger* – that's what's needed in a treasure hunt!'

'Danger?'

'Fellers with guts will come through it all right. Doesn't matter about the lily-livers, they won't be any loss – and what are you all hanging around here for with your gobs hanging open? Get cracking!'

Conversation on the way to Slidemaster Street tended to be rather stilted. Cathy felt too humiliated to say much, and Gillian and Barbara kept glancing at one another as though they wished now they hadn't come to her outlandish party. When they reached the police station she unfolded the first slip of paper with a sense of doom, and after reading the message written there, knew that her instincts had been right.

'What's it say?' Barbara asked curiously.

'Steal . . . steal a . . . '

'*Steal* something?'

'Um . . . steal a nail off the roof of the police station lock-up, actually,' Cathy muttered, red-faced.

There was a short, splintery silence.

'Treasure hunt instructions usually just lead from one place to another, then you find a nice little prize at the end,' Barbara said coldly. 'A chocolate frog or a pretty hair-ribbon, things like that.'

'Sergeant Jobey's inside the police station,' Gillian said. 'He's so scary, like a sheriff out of a Wild West film, that's why the crime rate's so low in this town. I don't suppose . . . I don't suppose he'd actually just *give* us a roofing nail if we went in there and asked . . . '

'He'd give us a boot up the backside,' Cathy said. 'The only way we could get that roofing nail is to nip down the side alley and climb over the fence.'

'We can't possibly!' Barbara said, scandalised. 'I don't mean to criticise your father, Cathy, but it's a very strange thing to expect birthday guests to do.'

'Well, we don't really have to play this game, you know. We could just . . . just go downtown and look in the shop windows instead,' Cathy said quickly, but to her surprise, Barbara and Gillian had edged away into the side alley. Cathy hesitated and went after them.

'Some of those roofing nails look a bit loose,' Gillian said, climbing the fence to examine the lock-up, which was a small brick shed with a barred window. 'They'd most likely come out with one tug – that's if anyone was silly enough to even . . . '

'I guess I could zip over and get one.'

'Cathy Melling, don't you dare, you'll get us all arrested!' Barbara cried behind them. 'And you've got your best dress on, Gillian, what will your mum say if you . . . '

'If you don't pipe down, you'll have Sergeant Jobey out here,' Cathy hissed. 'Shut up and let me concentrate. It shouldn't be all that hard getting one of those nails, and I wouldn't have to climb right down, either. You could just about reach over from the top of the fence . . . '

'It's very rude to grab the first turn at your own birthday party. I don't see why I can't have a go,' Gillian said unexpectedly, and pushed Cathy aside. She stepped over the nettle-filled gap and braced one foot on the window ledge, but as she began to prise at the nearest nail, someone suddenly reached out and grabbed her ankle.

'Give us a cuppa tea, love, and tell old Roy I'm his best mate and never meant to punch him . . . ' a voice croaked from behind the little barred window.

'Oh help!' Gillian squeaked. 'Quick, someone – poke the creepy old thing off with a stick!'

There was no stick handy, but Cathy said in her best threatening voice, 'Let go her foot! If the Sergeant comes out he'll think you're trying to escape – and you'll be stuck in there another night!'

The skinny claw and white stubble of whiskers

vanished from the window, and Gillian scrambled back across the gap and down into the alley.

'Not even dropping the roofing nail – that's what I call brave!' Barbara said admiringly.

'I was brave, wasn't I? Oooh, it was so *horrible*, that hand shooting out and grabbing my ankle – I nearly died!'

'And I nearly died when his voice came croaking out the window – I was thinking he could be a *murderer*!'

'Every other birthday party I've been to we played *proper* games like Pin-the-Tail and Sardines,' Gillian said, shuddering. 'I don't know what my mum's going to say when she finds out I've had an awful old murderer's hand all scaly like an emu's clutching my ankle!'

'It wasn't a murderer, it was only poor old Mr Wetherell from Conifer Crossing,' Cathy said. 'He comes into town once a week to get drunk and pick fights with people and Sergeant Jobey puts him in the lock-up to sleep it off. Look, Gillian, maybe you'd better chuck that dirty old nail away before you get rust all over your good dress . . . '

'Throw it away?' Gillian demanded incredulously. 'After all I went through to get it? I've never *ever* pinched anything from a police station lock-up before, and after we've shown it to your dad to prove we got it, I'm going to keep it for a souvenir . . . What's it say on the next bit of paper, Cathy?'

'I don't know and I don't care! Listen, we don't really have to do any of the other things. We could . . . well, go down to the park and see if there's anyone else we know there,' Cathy said, but Gillian had already snatched the next slip of paper and was reading it aloud.

' "Scoot round to Tavistell Street and swipe a peg from

the nuns' clothesline?" ' Barbara repeated, shocked. 'I certainly don't think we should be doing any such thing!'

'Neither do I,' Cathy said swiftly, thinking of school on Monday and how Barbara would blab to everyone that Cathy Melling's birthday party consisted of a disgraceful game all over town stealing items from the police station and the Convent. 'If you don't want to go to the park, how about a nice walk down by the river instead? Honest, we really don't have to chase about collecting all these stupid . . . '

'The Convent's not all that far away,' Gillian said. 'We could just sort of stroll around the back and – you know, have a bit of a look over the fence . . . '

'They haven't got a back fence you can look over, it's too tall,' Barbara said. 'It's made like that on purpose so people won't find out what goes on behind it.'

'Well, that's why I'd kind of like to see inside,' Gillian admitted, and Cathy eyed her in secret amazement, for that sleek, well-brushed head looked as though it would never contain such thoughts. The Convent fence, however, when they reached it, was not only too high to see over, but was topped with sharp little arrow spikes that cancelled any attempts at climbing.

'I'm not surprised,' Barbara said. 'I read somewhere you can't ever quit once you become a nun, even if you don't like it. Once they've got you in their clutches you never see the light of day ever again!'

'That can't be true, I've seen the nuns down at the shops on Saturday mornings a whole lot of times. And when Grace went away to the city there were two of them getting on the same train with suitcases. They even offered her a stick of barley sugar . . . '

'Doesn't prove anything,' Barbara said darkly. 'The ones on the train were probably trying to run away. And I bet they never got as far as the city, either – they would have been snatched off that train by force and brought back. Then they would have been walled up alive . . . Look! I told you so – there's a gap where the bricks join up with the paling fence next door. Some poor little desperate nun's obviously been out here late at night trying to escape, tearing the bricks out with her fingernails!'

'But that's always been like that,' Cathy said. 'That house next door started putting up a paling fence years ago and never finished the job. Lucky for us I suppose – we could squeeze through that gap, if we held our breath. You needn't come, Barb, if you'd rather not.'

But Barbara Sylvester, inexplicably, was the first one through the gap and even led the way through a grove of fruit trees on the other side. Beyond the orchard were vegetable beds, a small lawn with a clothesline, garden sheds, and a trellis bearing grapevines. When they reached the vegetable beds, a black-gowned nun suddenly popped out from nowhere with a wheelbarrow. They ducked down behind a huge spreading clump of rhubarb and watched as she began to rake fallen leaves into a heap. While she worked she chatted to someone else out of sight behind the grape trellis. Cathy listened, her mind ablaze with images of people being forced from trains, but the conversation seemed disappointingly ordinary, of the type anyone might have.

' . . . something's got to be done soon about lopping back this tree, the spouting's all choked up again . . . There I was, dough from the scones all over my hands and that wretched front doorbell kept ringing and ringing . . . The cupboard on the left, dear, and if it's not there, look under the . . . Borax might get it out, or salt . . . '

There was a background of other sounds, but they were quite ordinary, too: someone playing piano scales and making mistakes, a mat being flapped from an upstairs window, the thud of balls from the tennis court around the far side of the Convent. Cathy felt quite cheated, but the other two obviously felt as though they were getting their money's worth. Barbara's whole face was an exclamation mark, her lower lip sucked fearfully in behind her top teeth, and Gillian looked just as scared. But the nun, to Cathy's disappointment, did nothing more startling than dump the fallen leaves into the wheelbarrow and take it behind the trellis.

'I heard a door open and shut, so she's probably gone inside. If we want to get one of those pegs from the line, now's our chance – but I'm not volunteering. I don't see why we can't get a peg from just anywhere and pretend it's from the Convent. No one would even know the difference,' Cathy said, for Barbara and Gillian's jitteriness was infectious. The path to the clothesline somehow gave the illusion of seeming much longer than it actually was.

'Nuns' pegs probably have crosses or holy pictures carved on them to make them different,' Barbara said. 'And I just thought – maybe they've got concealed microphones hidden in this rhubarb patch and all over the garden, too!'

'Why on earth would they?'

'To make sure no one gets in here and tries to kidnap their relatives back, that's why! Someone could be listening in to every single word we say, and I bet they'll all come dashing out with a big net or something pretty soon. Just don't expect *me* to go and get that peg, either!'

'If I can climb the roof of a police lock-up and get grabbed by a murderer, I should think one of you could face up to a nun!' Gillian said smugly. 'They couldn't even run very fast in all those long skirts.'

'Are you by any chance hinting around that I'm a coward?' Barbara snapped.

'Well, I certainly didn't notice you volunteering about the roofing nail! But you don't have to worry – *I'll* go and get that peg, then I'll have *two* treasure hunt souvenirs . . . '

'You greedy thing, Gillian Ogden!' Barbara said angrily, and crept out from behind the rhubarb. She tiptoed across the lawn towards the clothesline, but a voice called sharply from behind the trellis, 'You bold little article, coming in here to raid our grapes! Get out of there this minute, they're all finished for the year, anyhow, so – *shoo!*'

Barbara swerved away wildly, but with great daring snatched a peg from the line as she fled. She pelted back through the orchard and caught up with Cathy and Gillian, who, having blatantly left her to her fate, were already squeezing through the gap in the fence. They ran all the way up Tavistell Street, which slumbered gently in the autumn sunlight, raced around into Curtain Street and fell in a disorganised heap behind the corner park bandstand.

'I've never been so petrified in my whole life!' Barbara gasped. 'It was *gruesome*! There was one of *them* sitting behind the trellis knitting – making out she was just like normal people, the sly old thing! There she was with the sun glinting on her specs like . . . like she had eyes made out of lava! Oh, I never thought I'd get away, I thought I'd be dragged inside that place and they'd make me put on a long black dress and sleep in a cell! But look here, just look what I got – a *real nun's peg* from the Convent garden!'

'It's just like everyone else's pegs,' Cathy said. 'An ordinary old wooden one with no holy markings at all.'

'You're just jealous! Here's Gillian with a nail from the police station and me nearly getting walled up alive with my peg – but you haven't even got a single solitary thing on this treasure hunt yet!'

Cathy, vastly annoyed, ripped open the last piece of paper and read, 'Fetch some kitchen lino out of the haunted house in River Road – watch out for banshees!'

'That place!' Gillian said. 'You wouldn't catch *me* going in there! It really *is* haunted – Marjorie Powell reckons she's seen mysterious lights moving about behind the windows at night.'

'It's just an old house falling to bits because no one lives in it,' Cathy said scornfully, getting up and brushing grass clippings from the seat of her pants. 'And as if anyone would believe anything Marjorie Powell says! She's the biggest liar in town. She told my sister she had a double-storey play-house in her backyard, and Viv went there on a message once, but there wasn't anything like that at all!'

'There's lots of other people besides Marjorie who've seen those lights after dark. That house is *so* haunted! I bet you wouldn't be game enough to go in there and get a piece of kitchen lino!'

'Those lights are only beery old tramps with matches and cigarette butts. I'm certainly not scared of an old house. And for your information I'll just march right in there and get a whole roll of lino if I feel like it! Naturally, I won't expect you two to come in with me if you're both so scared, you can just wait outside.'

Cathy swaggered confidently all the way down to River Road, but as they approached the old house by the river, her pace slackened. That house had been derelict for as long as she or anyone else could remember, every year settling deeper into the ground and shedding more of its fabric. Waiting on the footpath for the others to catch up, she noticed that the house stirred constantly in various ways. Grass rippled along the gutters, the entire tin roof vibrated gently, ancient ribbons of dried-up paint shivered in the breeze from the river.

'I'm glad it's *you* going inside that spooky old haunted house and not us!' Gillian said. 'There's kids at school who even cross over so they won't have to walk past it.'

'It only looks haunted because everyone acts like it is. Everyone's so stupid. I've been inside there heaps of times and nothing's happened.'

'You've been in *there*? All the way inside, no kidding?'

'Well . . . I went up to the front door once and banged the knocker,' Cathy conceded. 'But that still counts, because I stayed right there on the veranda and knocked a whole lot of times. No ghosts came out – the only thing was an old bird's-nest shook loose out of the fanlight and landed down my neck . . . ' She stopped, remembering suddenly a much smaller Cathy who'd leaped back, fallen off the veranda and then run all the way up the hill without stopping to draw breath. The composite parts of the house, she noticed apprehensively, didn't just move, but were quite noisy about it, creaking and rasping and murmuring amongst themselves. 'Actually, if you think about it, it probably isn't all that safe inside with everything rotting away to bits,' she added. 'People could easily fall through the floorboards and break their leg. This treasure hunt's kind of silly, really. How about we just go for a walk up to the blacksmith's and watch . . . '

'*Some* people seem to be backing out when it's *their* turn,' Barbara said. 'Specially the ones full of big talk . . . '

'You rotten liar, Barbara Sylvester! I am *not* trying to back out of anything!'

'Well, hurry up and get that lino, then! It's not very nice waiting around outside like this – anything could pop up behind one of those windows and stare out at us! Of course, if you're too nervous, we can just go back to your place and look at what you got for your birthday . . . '

Cathy, glaring, marched proudly up the overgrown path to the front door and shoved it open. It stopped half-way, teetering drunkenly on one rusty hinge. She set one foot over the threshold into the shadows, then withdrew it. The house seemed even more restless inside, as though some variety of life was active there, a secretive life manifesting itself in furtive rustlings . . . She jumped as a long stalactite of cobweb swung out and brushed across her face.

'What's up, what was it?' Gillian quavered from the gateway. 'Did you . . . *see* something?'

'Course not!' Cathy said resolutely and threaded her way through fallen plaster and split floorboards to what had once been a kitchen. There was a green twilight in there, for vines had smothered the broken window, curling thin arms over the sill. Cathy glanced at the vines, remembering a Tarzan film she'd once seen about vegetation that possessed an evil intelligence of its own and strangled people. She remembered other things – Stewart Thurlow swearing he'd passed this house and heard a blood-curdling scream choked off in the middle; Isobel claiming a large black leathery thing had come streaking from a window and flapped right past her ear; that old story about the skeleton found under the kitchen floorboards with a knife blade wedged between its ribs . . .

Cathy knelt to prise a scrap of lino from the floor. It clung stubbornly to its jute backing, refusing to break. As she worked away at it, a huge spider suddenly scuttled from a crack in the floor, raced across her hand and vanished under a pile of rubbish. Cathy, who had a phobia about spiders, screamed and tumbled backwards, holding the snapped piece of lino. She scrambled up and raced outside, still yelling. Barbara and Gillian screamed, too, and bolted away up the hospital hill, not waiting for her.

'Hang on a minute! There's no ghosts coming after us, it was only this big spider . . . ' Cathy called, but they still didn't stop, and went galloping over the crest of the hill and down the slope towards her house. Cathy sped after them, groaning, remembering that the worst was yet to come. Now they'd expect to be shown her marvellous secret birthday present which was supposed to be even better than a gold wristwatch! Her mind raced frantically over household items she could perhaps claim to be that present – Heather's brass statuette she'd got at the Show, Mum's big cedar chest, the plaster spaniel doorstop, the cow – maybe she could claim that Dad was setting her up with her very own dairy herd . . . And the present wasn't her only worry, for Barbara and Gillian were also expecting afternoon tea served on the ferry!

'Listen, wait a minute . . . there's something I forgot to mention,' she called desperately, but they'd already reached the side gate and were rushing over to Dad by the shed, waving their clothespeg and roofing nail. It was all his fault, Cathy thought morosely. He'd just made the whole thing worse than it was, and while she'd had to suffer all the humiliations of the afternoon, he'd been tinkering about peacefully in the shed . . . She shaded her eyes from the sun and peered at something propped on two kerosene drums, something sparkling with fresh paint.

'Just as well you went out gallivanting all over town with your mates. Gave me a chance to finish this off without you here poking your nose in. All it needed was sandpaper and a lick of paint . . . ' Dad said as Cathy advanced slowly across the yard, staring at a little blue rowboat, so minute and endearing it looked like something out of *The Wind in the Willows*.

'I found it cleaning out the shed when Aunt Ivy was here on the rampage. Must have been in there donkey's years by the look of things, slung up on the rafters under a load of old bags and rubbish,' Dad explained. 'You can be boss of it seeing you're so nuts about the river. Takes all kinds, I suppose – never fancied the navy much myself, cavalry's better.'

Cathy couldn't say anything. She put out a tender hand and traced the boat's name painted on the side in dashing letters.

'Oh, Cathy – your own little boat named after you!' Gillian said. 'You never even told us you were getting a ducky little rowboat for your birthday! Was that what you really meant by having afternoon tea on a ferry?'

'Try sitting in this ferry just yet and you'll end up with blue paint all over your breeches,' Dad said. 'Come back another day when it's dry and she might take you out fishing – she's pretty good at slinging a line.'

'Can you make up another treasure hunt for us then?' Barbara asked. 'That was the best one I've ever been on in my whole life!'

'Why can't we have another one right now?' Gillian said. 'Go on, Mr Melling!'

'Clear out,' Dad said. 'You can all just flap off now and give a bloke some peace. If there's one thing I can't stand, next to sooking, it's a mob of gabby little earbashing sheilas all over lace and frills and ribbons! Go on, bloody clear out the lot of you and find something else to do!'

'Don't mind him,' Cathy said. 'Let's go inside and have something to eat. There's beaut date-slice and tea – made specially with condensed milk seeing it's my birthday.'

'You lucky thing!' Barbara and Gillian said jealously. 'We *never* get condensed milk at home!'

# ♫ Dresses of Red and Gold

The little annexe off the main ward seemed to contain a permanent draught created by Nurse Durbach's zealous comings and goings. Her shoes squealed over the polished floor, she whisked towels away before people had finished with them, her voice crackled as starchily as hospital linen if anyone held her up for more than a minute. All that hectic charging about wasn't really necessary – she probably just felt important doing it, Vivienne decided.

'Last time you'll be needing a wash-basin now you're officially allowed up,' Nurse Durbach said, poised like a statue of Mercury to snatch the dish away almost before Vivienne had time to spit out the mouthwash. 'You shouldn't need help getting to the bathroom any more. Use that little one through the end door, only don't go making a racket and disturbing the lady in the other bed.'

The other bed was tucked away behind a screen, and its occupant hadn't uttered one word since Vivienne had been moved to the annexe that morning. It was much more pleasant than the main ward, for there was the garden to look at. When Nurse Durbach had whirled away to tackle a dozen other jobs, Vivienne gazed out at the lawn, carpeted gloriously with fallen leaves. Some had blown against the window panes, attaching themselves like a frieze of red and gold paper decorations. The window also overlooked the hospital driveway, busy now with people arriving for afternoon Visiting Hour. Mum, laden with packets and bundles, was amongst them, and when she finally found her way through all the rambling corridors to the annexe, she was flustered and inclined to drop them all. She'd brought a clean nightie, handkerchiefs, a bunch of everlasting daisies, two library books, an egg-timer she'd packed by mistake and a money-box Dad had made and sent down from Queensland where he'd gone to look for work. Vivienne was enchanted by it. It was shaped like a log cabin, with yellow glass windows giving an impression of miniature people gathered snugly around a fireside within. Nurse Durbach, racing afternoon tea trays around, clearly wasn't enchanted by such an object cluttering a bedside locker. She brushed up some slivers of bark, and obviously didn't think much of Mum's daisies, either. They were whizzed away to be put in a vase, but not brought back.

'It's a funny thing how that Durbach girl's grown up thinking she's just the cat's whiskers and Queen Mary rolled into one,' Mum said reflectively. 'I remember when old Sammy Durbach – that was her grandad – used to have a pie-run. He'd pedal around town ringing a bell on this rattle-trap old carrier bike. Saveloys, he used to sell, as well as pies, but you wouldn't have wanted to buy any.'

Vivienne grinned, pleased to find that it no longer hurt so much. 'Doctor Caulfield said I can go home in a couple of days,' she said. 'I'm glad it's all over – it was terrible!'

'Yes, I know, love, but you were a brave girl,' Mum

said. 'All you've got to do now is rest and let things heal in their own good time. They just about always do one way or another.'

Vivienne imagined her brain sending capable messages to nerves and tissue, saying, 'Okay now, you lot – settle down! No call for any more fuss, get on with what you're supposed to be doing!' and felt comforted.

'How come they've moved you out of the big ward?' Mum asked. 'I just about leaned down and smooched a perfect stranger before I even realised.'

'Short of space in there, but I don't mind, it's nicer out here. There's even a little bathroom up that end, though I guess I'm supposed to share it with the lady in the other bed. Only I don't know if she's allowed up yet, she's been asleep ever since they moved me out here.'

'No one's turned up to visit her yet. I wonder if she's got anyone at all to bring in clean nighties and see to her messages – maybe I'd just better go and . . . '

'It's *me* you've come to visit,' Vivienne protested, concluding suddenly that her brain wasn't sending healing messages quite fast enough. And also, she noticed, Cathy hadn't bothered to get any of the library books on the list she'd sent home. Cathy's selection looked awful, one cover showing a girl on horseback rounding up cattle, the other a ship being attacked by a huge sea monster. 'Anyhow, if there's a screen up round a bed it means they're feeling poorly and the nurses want them getting plenty of rest. Ow, my throat *hurts*, Mum! I've got this horrible taste in my mouth and it won't go away. They keep making me get up and walk around even though my legs go all buckled, and I want to go home . . . '

'Stop grousing,' Mum said. 'Anyone would think

no one else ever had their tonsils out before. And if you don't stop whingeing, that girl Durbach mightn't let you have any of her grandad's nice saveloys for tea.'

But tea, arriving an hour after Mum had left, was pallid scrambled egg, strawberry junket and bossy instructions from Nurse Durbach to eat every mouthful. Vivienne sat up against pillows pummelled to the consistency of sand-bags and didn't dare disobey, even though she hated both scrambled eggs and junket. The lady in the next bed appeared to loathe them, too, for after ten minutes of coaxing, Nurse Durbach came out from behind the screen with an untouched tray.

'That dinner wasn't very nice, was it?' Vivienne said shyly in the direction of the next bed when Nurse Durbach had gone, but received no answer. She got up, feeling heroic on her wobbly legs, and followed the autumn leaf frieze along the row of windows, past the other bed and into the bathroom. There was an alarming moment when the floor in there seemed to swell and curl like a wave, making her cling to the basin till things righted themselves.

She tottered slowly back to bed, grasping the window ledge. It was growing dark outside now, and the big amber lights had been switched on above the hospital entrance. That lady in the other bed had been very quiet and uncomplaining all day behind her screen. It felt peculiar sharing a room with someone you couldn't see, even if it wasn't really a proper room, just a little closed-in veranda. Vivienne glanced at the screen as she passed, observing this time that one of the shirred panels had puckered up, leaving a gap. It was like looking at a picture composed almost entirely in white, she thought, peering through the gap – silvery locks of hair spread over a pillow, elderly skin like furrowed cream, a white bedspread rising and falling so imperceptibly you had to look closely to make sure it was even moving.

'You keep over your own side of the room, Miss Sticky-beak!' Nurse Durbach said acidly from the doorway.

'I was only . . . I just . . . ' Vivienne stammered, retreating to her bed with two spots of colour burning in her cheeks like aces.

'As soon as you're allowed up, you kids always make little pests of yourselves – and don't dump your dressing-gown on the bed like that, either! This happens to be a hospital, not the playground down at the park. Fold your dressing-gown over the back of the chair when you're not using it. If there's one thing I can't stand the sight of it's a messy ward!'

Vivienne, too intimidated to move in case she got into any more trouble, sat perfectly still until evening Visiting Hour brought Heather, Cathy and Isobel, but not Mum this time, because the hospital allowed three visitors only at a time. The poor old lady in the next bed, she noticed sympathetically, still didn't have even one.

'Pity you didn't have a smarter nightie,' Isobel said, helping herself to a slab of the Turkish Delight she'd brought as a gift. 'Fancy Aunty Con expecting you to wear that flannelette thing with the piping gone all runny in the wash!'

'Trust you to make some remark about it,' Heather said crossly. 'No one sees nighties, not when you're stuck in bed, and Mum already had to buy her a new dressing-gown and slippers.'

'If I had to have an operation I'd get everything in oyster satin with matching feathery slippers,' Isobel said. 'Actually, I wouldn't mind a stay in hospital all that much. It must be kind of exciting, all those doctors strolling around in white jackets just like in a film.'

'Well, I've only ever noticed Doc Caulfield,' Vivienne said. 'And he hasn't got a white jacket, just his ordinary suit with the fob-watch.'

'I'm really surprised Aunty Connie let that old dodderer yank your tonsils out. He's so far gone he should be in here as a patient himself. You should have got that gorgeous new young one, Doctor MacNeill, the one who looks just like something out of a Foreign Legion film . . . '

'But we've always gone to Doc Caulfield, right from when we were all born. Grace is even named after him.'

'His first name's Grace?'

'Don't be silly,' Heather said. 'It's Robert, that's why she's got Roberta for her middle name. And he pulled Cathy through that time they thought she might have rheumatic fever, and there's when Dad got gored by the bull. Doctor Caulfield's not an old dodderer, he's lovely! He told Mum not to worry about the bill for Viv's tonsils till Dad finds a job.'

'Doctor MacNeill's lovelier,' Isobel said. 'With a bit of luck he might still be here when I leave school. I'm half thinking of being a nurse, you know – I reckon I'd look pretty good in one of those starchy veils.'

'Only the sisters have those. You have to do three years' training first and get bossed around something shocking – we learned all about it at Guides when we did First Aid. Anyway, I somehow can't see you fetching bedpans and holding bowls for people to be sick in.'

'There might be ways to dodge that part. Maybe I could talk them into letting me work just in the operating theatre and wear one of those cute mask things. I bet a certain doctor – and I certainly don't mean old Pop Caulfield – would get so he wouldn't even start operating unless I was in there helping!'

'Just as well Viv's already had her tonsils out, then,' Cathy said. 'This is a nice little room they've moved her to, better than that big ward with all the wailing little brats down one end. Just two beds – aren't we posh! Who's in that other one behind the screen?'

'A really old lady, but I don't know her name and I don't think I've ever seen her around town before,' Vivienne said, lowering her voice. 'I guess she must be pretty sick. They always seem to be popping in there to check up on her.'

'Just like in a film,' Isobel said enviously. 'I bet I could do nursey things like taking people's pulses, too, if someone showed me how.'

'Heather already did once, but you said you hated the feel of it, even your own. I don't see that you'd be much use as a nurse if you come out in goose pimples taking pulses.'

'It's probably not all that important. If a pulse thumps it means the person's alive and kicking, and if it's conked out then they have, too, and there's not much anyone can do about it. I expect nurses just take pulses to fill in the time when they're bored. As a matter of fact I'm bored right now just sitting here. Let's go round the corridors and see if there's anyone with an interesting-looking disease . . . '

'If you're hoping to catch a glimpse of Doctor MacNeill, you'll be disappointed. They only do their rounds in the mornings,' Vivienne said, but Isobel had already gone, taking Cathy and Heather with her. Slightly insulted at being left alone, she reached for the Turkish Delight but found that all gone, too. They were so mean, she thought self-pityingly, coming in to visit but then trotting off to goggle at other patients instead! And eating all her Turkish Delight, not even caring that she'd had her tonsils out and suffered terrible agony. Although the agony had dwindled now to something that could really only be called discomfort, she suspected that the inside of her throat must look quite dramatic if she could bring herself to take a look. If they'd been Cathy's tonsils, she thought, Cathy would have lost no time in getting the mirror out of the bedside locker, probably straight after she'd come back from the operating theatre. Most likely she would have demanded a magnifying glass, too, but Vivienne had faint-hearted qualms about personally examining Doctor Caulfield's handiwork for at least six months.

She scrunched the empty Turkish Delight bag into an indignant wad, then remembered that the only wastepaper basket was in the bathroom and that Nurse Durbach fizzled like static if you messed up her immaculate locker tops. She needed to go to the bathroom, anyway, and it would serve certain people right if they came back to find her bed mysteriously empty! They might think she'd had a relapse and been rushed off to the theatre again. Vivienne took her time in the bathroom, and tiptoeing past the screen on her way back, she was halted by a quavering thread of voice. The voice tripped over itself and mumbled into silence, but had sounded questioning. She hesitated, then put her head around the screen. Milky blue eyes glittered at her disconcertingly from the pillow. She had the odd impression that all the old lady's energies had drained from her body to lodge there instead, just behind her eyes.

'Er . . . can I get you anything?' Vivienne asked.

'Came right up to the front door, bold as brass . . .

Madness . . . Polly was going by, too – Polly Cleese, that is, not the Atkinson one . . . My goodness, chest so tight I can't . . . can't breathe.'

'Would you like me to ring for the nurse? I'm Vivienne, they moved me out here because the big ward was full up and they're rushed off their feet. Vivienne Melling, from Sawmill Road and I had my tonsils out.'

'Polly, she promised not to tell . . . Can't trust . . . Would you go down the lane a little way, just to the corner, he might be . . . '

'Yes, all right,' Vivienne said helplessly, and crept away, back to the sanctuary of her bed. Nurse Durbach, she thought, could cope with that poor old rambling thing with her feverish eyes which, in spite of their intensity, didn't even see things properly any more. She listened, but the troubled whispering had ceased. Cathy, Heather and Isobel came back as the bell signalled the end of Visiting Hour, pinkly subdued after having been told off by Nurse Durbach for roaming at large around the hospital. Isobel, apparently, had pried into a storage cupboard, creating an avalanche of splints, crutches and what she claimed had been a stockpile of artificial legs.

'So it's all *her* fault,' Heather said angrily, grabbing yesterday's nightie to take home for laundering. 'The utter embarrassment – all those things spilling out – one of the legs rolled along the corridor and tripped someone up! Just don't expect to see me in here again, I'd be too humiliated to show my face! If you need anything in particular, you'd better tell me quick and Mum or Cathy can bring it in tomorrow.'

'Ta ta, Viv, hope you make it through the night okay,' Isobel said. 'It's a funny thing about tonsil operations. One minute you can feel all bouncy – but one little attack of the coughs and you could be looking at your own reflection in a lake of blood all over the floor. Cheer up, though, I'm sure that lovely Doctor MacNeill would know what to do.'

Vivienne, alarmed, took care not to cough or even mildly clear her throat through the routine of being settled for the night. She was drowsily aware of the night nurses coming on duty much later, of someone tiptoeing into the annexe and shining a torch first in her direction, then behind the screen. There were other distractions, also: a phone ringing somewhere down the corridor, cars passing occasionally along River Road, boughs tapping against the window. She dozed fitfully, longing for her own bed and the comforting presence of Cathy nearby, of Mum just up the hall. The old lady tucked away behind the screen was a poor substitute. In spite of willpower, a tickle developed in her throat, and remembering Isobel's dire warning, she sat up hastily and sipped barley water. From behind the screen came small rustles and sighs – the old lady was awake, too.

'Do you want one of the night nurses? If you can't manage the buzzer, I'll press mine,' Vivienne said.

'All these years I didn't break as much as one cup from that good dinner-service. Not so much as a handle smashed! He'll always check – every time company comes and it's brought out, he'll check later. I put a rubber mat in the bowl and wash every single piece myself, bit by bit. Such a worry. Hands shake. I could . . . could accidentally drop . . . '

'My mum's always dropping things,' Vivienne said chattily. 'She's already gone through most of the dinner-set Aunty Cessie gave her Christmas before last.'

'Beautiful fine china. Gold rim. Such a worry and bother, Father always goes to the cabinet and checks.

Hateful old man! I'm very tired . . . never used to get tired . . . '

'If you're tired, you should be asleep,' Vivienne hinted.

'I'd better stop talking and let you . . . '

'Hateful, selfish old man! He stopped us. But he didn't know . . . I got away, I went dancing in the rain! Soaking-wet flowers from the hedge, we made them up into garlands. "You dear darling!" I said. "Why do you wear that funny thing on your head? Oh, you always look so handsome in your funny hat!" My word, dancing by the river, raining, we didn't care . . . Clay all over my good shoes, not fit to be seen. Had to . . . had to scrape all the red clay off in the garden so Father wouldn't know we . . . '

'It's really late now,' Vivienne said, but the old lady was fast asleep between one rasping word and the next.

Next morning Doctor Caulfield brought a little gift, a puzzle of two linked nails, but became interested in it himself and sat on the edge of Vivienne's bed till he'd managed to work it out. The Sister stood by glancing disapprovingly at her watch, but Doctor Caulfield didn't take any notice. He cheered Vivienne immensely by saying that her tonsils had been the largest ever known to medical science and he'd had to rig up a block and tackle to get the left side one out. Then he went behind the screen, staying in there a long time. His voice was unhurried and gentle, even though the old lady didn't seem to have the slightest idea who he was. She kept muttering querulously that she had to meet someone and where was her silk shawl with the bird pattern.

Morning tea arrived, then lunch, and afterwards an enforced nap. Vivienne did the nail puzzle under the bed-clothes instead, because Cathy's library books had proved unreadable after the first few pages. Then she entertained herself by watching the leaves fall outside the annexe window. Some spiralled down to join the window-pane frieze, others drifted out across the lawn, some clung stubbornly to their stalks even when tugged by a strong gust of wind. There seemed to be some unfathomable pattern in the sequence of their falling. Autumn leaves would make beautiful dresses, she thought idly, if they could only be preserved and stitched together. Such garments would be breathtaking – a rich gold and red fabric that would rustle at the wearer's every movement. Mum would certainly be overjoyed if clothes could be made as cheaply as that. Vivienne felt guilty every time she glanced at the new dressing-gown draped over the back of the chair. There'd been no time to run one up from an old coat or skirt, and it was unthinkable to go to hospital without a dressing-gown. If Nurse Durbach was on Admissions, she probably wouldn't even let you in the front door without one!

Cathy came alone at afternoon Visiting Hour, because Mum had some crisis with a broken denture, but Cathy was good company today. She invented a lively game of scribbles, all the drawings having to be connected somehow with hospitals. The old lady in the next bed slept through that episode of giggling silliness and through dinner, too, even though Sister herself went in there and tried to coax her to eat. She slept all through evening Visiting Hour, though Mum, denture repaired temporarily with woodwork glue, overstayed the bell by fifteen minutes to make up for not coming in the afternoon. When she'd gone, the annexe seemed bleak. It would have been nice, Vivienne thought forlornly, to have someone in the next bed who would chat, someone who didn't just lie there floating in and out of consciousness behind a white screen.

But later that evening there was a flurry of activity behind the screen. The junior nurse, who'd gone in there to settle the old lady for the night, came out again and fetched Sister, who summoned young Doctor MacNeill. Isobel, Vivienne thought, would be very disappointed to know that she'd missed him. She tried not to listen to the conversation, which wasn't meant for her ears, anyway, for Sister's voice, which could normally carry the whole length of a corridor, was confined to a whisper. Vivienne caught fragments of it while piecing together the lurid sunset of a jigsaw puzzle which Danny O'Keefe, astoundingly, had given Mum to bring to her in hospital.

'Doctor Caulfield's been called out to one of the farms, so . . . No relatives, poor old soul . . . up and down, rallying one minute and . . . Doctor Caulfield's had her on . . . very little more we can do for the moment . . . not really much point trying to . . .'

Doctor MacNeill came out again and smiled with such breezy charm at Vivienne that she almost forswore her loyalty, but then he ruined it all by saying in passing, 'How are things going, young Jeanette – how's the poor leg?'

Sister turned off the annexe light after confiscating the jigsaw puzzle and tucking the blankets in so firmly that Vivienne felt like a herring being sealed into a tin. She lay awake listening to the eleven o'clock staff change, with Nurse Durbach beginning a stint of night shift and apparently throwing her weight about as soon as Sister left. There seemed to be more torch rounds than usual, and Vivienne wished she could give up all attempts at sleep and read instead. The gentle illumination from the outside garden light was too faint for that, but it was pointless to ask Nurse Durbach if she could turn the bedside light on in the middle of the night. She lay awake listening to the small, subdued sounds of the hospital. The nurses were making themselves supper in the little room down the corridor. Each time the swing door opened, she could hear the chink of cups and snippets of their talk.

'Sister said Miss Bradtke's got to be checked every half-hour, and ring through to the nurses' home if . . . '

'Did you remember to check up about that duodenal having . . . '

'Don't look at *me*, Arnold was supposed to . . . '

'Oh, who's the dill put this biscuit-tin lid on so tight – can't even budge the damn thing!'

'Durbach – she had a proper clean-up in here, reckoned it was a pigsty. A whole *month* of her we've got, God help us . . . '

There was another faint conversation taking place nearby, but Vivienne, eavesdropping on the nurses from a distance, didn't at first realise that the old lady was awake and talking to herself. The words had long spaces between them, as though they were being dredged up from under-water, like shells or pearls. Vivienne wondered if she should press the buzzer; everyone had seemed concerned about that old lady earlier on, but how stupid she'd look if everything was perfectly all right and she'd called for nothing. Nurse Durbach would think her a nosey little pest, interfering in hospital business.

'Houseboat. Mountains. Reflected in the . . . in the lake. Flowers. When . . . when we get there we'll . . . '

Vivienne got up reluctantly and looked around the screen. 'Can't you sleep, either?' she asked, but received no answer. The old lady's eyes were shut and her hands plucked at the bedspread as though searching for something. Vivienne edged around the screen and tried to tuck those hands back under the covers, but found her own grasped. It seemed rude to draw back, even though the grasp was so weak it felt as though a butterfly had settled lightly on her wrist.

'India,' said the old lady.

'That's a long way away.'

'A long road. A long old rocky walk it's been . . . Tired . . . '

'You won't have to walk anywhere for a while,' Vivienne said. 'All you've got to do is stay in bed and let things heal in their own good time. Like they just about always do one way or another.'

'Dancing by the river. Such dark eyes . . . '

Vivienne, trying to stabilise the conversation, shared her idea of how you could perhaps make dresses from autumn leaves if only someone could think of a way to preserve them, but she didn't think the old lady heard.

'He said . . . Train. Next time he came we'd take . . . '

'Maybe I'd better ring for the nurse,' Vivienne said hastily, not wishing to be responsible for someone who kept drifting away to some other time and place. It was like having to keep an eye on a boat that had cast its mooring, she thought. Just like the time she'd stood by the riverbank and watched helplessly as Cathy's little boat floated down towards the ferry-crossing. The rumpus Cathy had made afterwards – and it hadn't even mattered, anyhow, for the boat had just drifted a short way downstream and come to rest, unharmed, in a quiet bend of the river.

'My sister got this tiny little boat for her birthday,' she said brightly, trying to moor the old lady's restlessness with words. 'Dad found it in the shed and fixed it up as a surprise. It's lovely, all painted blue. Heather and Cathy go out fishing in it, only I have to sit on the bank and watch because I can't swim properly yet.'

'Such dark eyes. Velvet . . . '

Vivienne fidgeted, needing desperately to go to the bathroom, but not liking to take her hand away. The old lady's voice was getting smaller and dimmer, like a lantern being carried away up a hill. Perhaps she'd stop meandering soon and go back to sleep. Vivienne yawned, listening to the hospital noises, which suddenly seemed to have changed tempo and grown busier. Someone came hurrying up the corridor from the maternity ward and whispered sharply, 'I don't *care*! Tell Durbach she's got to come herself, not just send us down that stupid junior! Sylvester's run off her feet trying to cope, and . . . What the heck do you think we've been doing, woman – playing hopscotch? No one's even answering at his place, so Syl rang . . . ' Doors swished open and shut and someone wheeled a trolley at speed the whole length of the corridor. Vivienne detached her hand and went to the door to listen for a while.

'I think someone might be having a baby, and they're having trouble,' she said importantly over her shoulder. 'They're all rushing around like mad down there! There's a car coming up the hill, too, sounds like Doctor Caulfield's rattly old thing . . . but I guess he's used to being woken up all hours.'

The old lady didn't answer. Vivienne suddenly had a craving for a hot drink of some kind to sip luxuriously in bed. It would be thoughtless to press the buzzer and ask while everyone seemed so busy with that emergency down in the maternity ward, but perhaps no one would mind if she went into the little corridor room and made it herself. She'd noticed other patients do that, stroll in there and make themselves cups of tea and Milo. Perhaps the old lady in the next bed would like one, too, it might help her rest soundly through what was left of the night.

She went behind the screen, but the old lady had already fallen asleep, one arm dangling over the side of the bed. Vivienne began to tuck it gently back under the bedspread, then halted. She took one frightened step backwards, and stood very still, gripping the edge of the screen.

Someone . . . I'd better ring for someone, she thought. But if they're all down that other end, they mightn't hear! Better go along the corridor and call those nurses, even though they're so busy . . . tell them that one of the patients . . . that she's . . .

Suddenly she wanted Mum so badly she thought she would run out of the annexe, across the lawn carpeted in leaves and down the hill towards home, run away from the fear that was swamping her now. A deserted road at night, all in darkness, was nothing compared to standing here quite alone, with a person who'd just . . . But after that quick instinctive step backwards, she couldn't make her feet obey her. They anchored her to the floor, forced her to stand there staring dazedly, staring at the bed.

Vivienne became aware of something strange. The old lady, although she still lay there, in some mysterious fashion had gone completely away. She simply wasn't there at all, but appeared to have slipped very quietly and gently out of the room. Whatever lay there didn't really seem to have anything to do with her at all. It was just like . . . like a shawl, Vivienne thought, astonished, an article of clothing finished with and left behind because it was no longer needed.

I should call someone, she thought more calmly,

emerging from her terror like a diver coming up for air. Nurse Durbach, she's in charge when Sister's not around . . .

But in the quiet room, with the last of the leaves whispering down to settle on the window ledge, she thought that perhaps there was no great urgency. In fact, there didn't seem to be any need whatsoever for Nurse Durbach with all her hurry and rush, no urgency at all. '

## ℐ Moving On

The ghastliness of having to share a room again, even for three nights, with irritating little sisters! Heather thought, trying to find space for her clothes. She scooped an armful of unidentifiable cardboard oblongs from the top drawer and hurled them through the door at Cathy, who said indignantly, 'Watch it – that happens to be my Welcome Home banner for Grace. I was just about to pin it up out the front.'

'Hypocrite – I seem to remember you wanted to make a Good Riddance one when she left! And you're only hanging that up because you think she'll be bringing you back a present from the city,' Heather scoffed and went stomping out to the kitchen, where Mum, wearing the blouse that made her look like a large floral clock, was basting a roast.

'I was thinking – maybe I should whip up a batch of Yorkshire pudding just in case,' Mum said. 'Men never think a roast is a proper one unless there's Yorkshire pudding to go with it – but then again, Grace never said anything in her letter about inviting Anthony Robinson in for tea. Just that he'd offered to meet her train and give her a lift home. What a nice, thoughtful young man . . . '

'Probably had no choice,' Heather said indifferently. 'Grace most likely ordered him to, she always did treat him like something squishy she'd just trodden in. Fancy *her* having an old flame – even if it's just Anthony Robinson with his big curly ears. Forget about the Yorkshire pudding, he'll have picked her up by now and they'll be on their way.'

'Oh dear, I wish Grace had *said*. It's such a tiny roast, too, barely enough for all you girls, and a wicked extravagance at that. Maybe if I cut all the potatoes in half and made extra gravy . . . '

'Mum, stop fussing! He's not likely to even *want* to come in, anyhow, after twenty minutes of Grace's company in the car. Bossy stuck-up hag she is, I can't understand why he's still interested. You'd think he'd have found someone else since she went off to the city.'

'That's not a very nice way to talk about your own sister, Heather. And another thing – I hope you shifted all your things out of her room like you were told to.'

'Yes I *did* – and it's not even fair! Expecting *me* to be inconvenienced just because Her Highness decided to come home for a few days! Having to muck in with Cathy and Viv – and muck's exactly the right word, too! You should see all the apple cores under Cathy's bed! I can't believe how revolting it's got since Aunt Ivy made her clean it out last month. It's just not fair that Grace . . . '

'I don't want to hear any more of your grizzling, young lady. You're doing far too much of it lately for my liking. That room's only been on loan and you'll have to give it back, anyway, when Grace finishes her dressmaking course and comes home for good . . . wherever we happen to be living then,' Mum said, suddenly looking very unfestive in spite of the cheerful blouse.

Heather, too cross to lend a sympathetic ear to that particular problem, took herself off to the veranda, wanting, for devious reasons of her own, to be the first person to see Grace arrive. She planned to nod coolly, say 'Oh . . . hello, I forgot it was today you were coming', then stroll away inside and put her nose in a book for the rest of the evening. But Vivienne and Cathy, perched on the gateposts with the banner held between them, had already set up a wild yell of welcome as Anthony Robinson's Austin came over the hill. Mum came rushing outside, bright-eyed with emotion, and instantly forgot all about Anthony being invited for tea or not. When she finished hugging Grace and did remember, he'd already put the suitcase on the veranda and taken himself shyly off.

'Oh, you've lost weight, love, you're thin as a rake! I bet you haven't been eating properly in the city,' Mum said, gazing besottedly at Grace as though something might spirit her away before she was safely inside and sitting down at the table. Heather, who had spent much time lately despairing over her own puppy fat, eyed Grace's trim waistline with jealousy. She'd forgotten how elegant Grace could look, even on limited means, how she could somehow make you feel as though you hadn't brushed your hair for a week, or had a spot on your chin even though you knew there wasn't one there at all.

'What did you bring us?' Cathy demanded. 'Can we have our presents right now?'

'Cathy, that's very greedy and rude! Leave your poor sister alone until she's had something to eat,' scolded Mum, who believed that any train trip was a daunting ordeal and travellers should be nurtured immediately afterwards.

'I'll get changed first,' Grace said. 'This jacket took ten years off my life to make and I don't want to get marks on it. But they can come and watch me unpack if they like.'

Heather hesitated, then followed at a distance, because that invitation was of the patronising variety people were inclined to toss at children. But *she* wasn't a child any longer – surely Grace had noticed how mature she'd become in the past five months? She'd experienced things – secretly examined all the illustrations in the *Home Medical Journal* Mum kept hidden in the sideboard, sneaked off with Isobel to see a travelling-tent performance called 'Murphy's Follies', even though everyone thought she'd gone to a special Guide meeting ... And this year she'd been to the Show with a *boy* – even if it was only that galoot Dennis Stivens whose hobby was still making balsa wood aeroplanes! Five months was a long time, long enough for a considerable shifting of position to have taken place within a family. No one could possibly include her in the same category as Viv and Cathy any longer! She hovered aloofly in the door-way, hoping that Grace would look up from unpacking and say, 'I can't really expect you to move back out with the little kids just because of me, Heather. How about bringing a mattress in here, then we can have a good old gossip tonight?'

'What's all this arty stuff in your port – sketch-books and paints and pencils?' Cathy asked. 'If that's supposed to be my present, you're going to get it slung right back at you for Christmas!'

'Don't touch! They're mine, I've enrolled in an art class as well as that dressmaking thing,' Grace said, quickly retrieving the sketch-pad before anyone could look inside, but Cathy's attention, flighty at the best of times, was already riveted upon something else.

'Where'd you get that silver charm bracelet?' she asked. 'You never had that when you went away . . . '

'It was a birthday present. Anthony Robinson sent it to me.'

'Sent you a real silver charm bracelet with a heart dangling from it?'

'Why shouldn't he?' Grace said equably, and distributed her own gifts brought from the city. Heather felt vaguely dissatisfied with the writing-folder she'd been given, because Grace had bought identical ones for Cathy and Vivienne. It was as though she'd seen a display of them in some shop and thought, 'Aha, just the thing to take home for the children!'

Mum was delighted with her gift of a new handbag, and kept it by her all through the meal, with a pleasure monumental enough to make Heather feel even more discontented. She wished she could be the one returning from the city with grand presents, that someone had given *her* a pretty silver bracelet with a heart charm. The only gift she'd ever received from an admirer was a brass statuette Dennis Stivens had won at the hoopla stall, and she suspected he'd given it to her only because he didn't want to be seen carting it around all afternoon at the Show. Enviable, citified Grace, with her self-confidence and polished table-manners . . .

'I notice we've still got this dreadful cutlery with the handles gone all yellow,' Grace said. 'Cathy, you should put your knife and fork side by side when you finish, it looks uncouth leaving them crossed like that.'

'Ho hum – just like old times, getting picked on at the table,' Cathy said, and she and Vivienne, the novelty of Grace's return now having diminished a little, set up a tiresome argument about whether the cutlery handles were ivory or bone.

Heather didn't join in their bickering. In the past she'd often been raucous on purpose just to irritate Grace, but now felt oddly subdued in her presence. She remained silent, consoling herself with another helping of steamed pudding and custard.

'I hope hordes of relations aren't going to be dropping in while I'm home,' Grace said, not having any of the steamed pudding at all, but finishing the meal with a pear. 'I mean . . . it's not that I don't want to see them, but I probably won't be in all that much, Mum. Margaret Edwards and that crowd I used to go out with have arranged a few things and I couldn't very well say no.'

'Well, Aunt Ivy's bound to want to see you, and so will Cessie, but it's only natural you'd like to catch up with your own friends first,' Mum said. 'It's such a pity you can't stay longer, dear. Only three days – and the last one doesn't really count, because you'll be going back in the afternoon. I just hope Dad makes it home in time to see you, he'll be disappointed if . . . '

'I explained all that in my letter,' Grace said patiently. 'Mr Quiller won't let anyone take holidays just any old time, you've got to wait till you've been there a full year. We've only got these few days off because the office is getting painted and rewired. No one can move without tripping over things, so that old skinflint asked us all to take time out of our annual holidays now. It's a nerve, really – you can't call autumn holiday weather, it's much too cold to go to the beach or anything. And we're expected back on Thursday, so that's all there is to it. That job might not be much, but I can't afford to be playing ducks and drakes with it.'

'I wish you'd just kept on at the daytime dressmaking course, instead of changing to night classes and juggling a job at the same time.'

'It didn't work out, Mum, I already told you. I hated having to ask Aunty Elsie for money every time I needed new stockings. Though, mind you, I get sick to death of that warehouse office, too. Everyone there is so stodgy – they've all been with R. T. Quiller and Son for about forty years! They've all got their own special teacups and have a fit if anyone else dares to touch them. Or even if you accidentally hang your coat up on *their* pegs in the wash-room – though all the pegs are exactly the same. You should see them when young Mr Quiller comes trotting in with a stack of invoices, their necks go pink and mottled – even though *he's* about sixty! Oh, those *depressing* invoices, all I do all day is stuff them in envelopes and put them through a franking machine. Thank goodness I won't have to be stuck in a job like that for the rest of my life! Soon as I get through that tech. course I'm going to . . . '

'Grace . . . ' Mum said diffidently. 'You know Miss Tully who makes clothes for all the ladies over in East Wilgawa?'

'The old dear who made Hilary's wedding dress?'

'And Cathy's bridesmaid one that Vivienne ended up wearing – but we won't go into that again now . . . Well, I heard Miss Tully's thinking of taking on a fulltime assistant. If you were to go and see her while you're home, I think she'd jump at the chance of getting you.'

It was impossible to tell from Grace's face if she were enthusiastic about the idea or not. She pushed the pear seeds into a complicated pattern on her plate and didn't say anything.

'I know you're only half-way through that course, but the rest is only practical, isn't it, making up set garments and having them marked? Perhaps you could come to some arrangement with the college, send them in by mail and still get your certificate. It seems a shame to pass up the chance of a good steady job, when they're so hard to come by in Wilgawa . . . '

Mum's not saying what she really means, Heather thought uncomfortably – that if Grace was home again and paying board, we might be able to hang on to this house for a little while longer. Grace will understand, though, without being actually told. She's the clever one in this family, never has to have things spelled out for her. If she came home again right now and got a job, Mum wouldn't have to worry so much. Mightn't be so bad . . . It'll mean I'd be stuck out in the back room with Cathy and Viv for ever, but I could learn a lot having Grace around. Watching her, how she talks and manages to get her hair looking like that, all smooth and shiny as moonlight . . .

'Well . . . ' Grace said. 'It's not exactly what I had in mind, sitting in Miss Tully's little work-room putting white piping in navy-blue yokes all day long. I remember when she used to come to school sometimes to fill in for the regular sewing teacher, the boring ideas she used to come up with – if you could even call them ideas! I bet Hilary had to give her step-by-step directions to get what she wanted for her bridesmaid dresses. I don't know, Mum. There are other things I'd much . . . '

'I'm sure she'd pay you just as much as what you're getting at that warehouse place. And you wouldn't even have the expense of bus fares, you could get down there by bike. Your old bike's still out in the shed. Cathy buckled the wheels a bit riding round the paddocks even though she's been told not to, but I'm sure Dad will be able to fix them when he comes home.'

'Er . . . one of the pedals is down the bottom of the brickworks quarry,' Cathy said guiltily. 'It was Danny O'Keefe, anyway, shoving a stick in the spokes. I'll get it back, Grace, soon as I get the chance to nip down there when the caretaker isn't around.'

Grace, astonishingly, didn't make any fuss, even though she'd chained her bike to a post in the shed before she'd left, with ferocious threats for anyone who dared lay a finger on it in her absence. She seemed far more interested in the pattern on her plate. 'I thought I'd be down at Aunt Elsie's till November at least,' she said.

'But . . . that's six months away,' Mum said slowly.

'I know, but as well as finishing off that course, there are . . . well, other things in the city I've got involved with. Friends I've made there . . . '

'You've got oodles of friends back here in Wilgawa,' Mum said. 'Eleanor Grantby and the two Edwards girls and all those others from when you belonged to the social club. People you went to school with and grew up with. It's a shame, having to board in the city away from all your old friends and away from . . . your own family. But if you went to work for Miss Tully . . . '

Heather, glancing at Mum, suddenly realised just how deeply Grace had been missed, and that any question of helping out with board money was really beside the point.

'I'll have a think about it,' Grace said non-committally. 'I mean, even if I decided to take it on, I'd still have to go back until Mr Quiller got someone to replace me. That's if I even ... oh, is that cup meant for me? I should have said I don't drink tea any more.'

'Not want a cup of tea?' Mum demanded, flabbergasted.

'Isn't there any coffee?'

'Only that coffee and chicory syrup Dad has sometimes when he's home. Coffee's supposed to be terrible for the complexion, Grace, and you've lost enough colour already living down there in the city.'

'I meant proper coffee, not that foul chicory stuff. I always drink it after dinner now instead of tea. Aunt Elsie's got these tiny coffee cups with gold rims – I nearly brought a set back for you.'

'I'm quite happy with my lovely new handbag,' Mum said. 'Only you shouldn't have spent anything on presents, it's enough to have *you* back home again. Oh, I wish the train fare wasn't so expensive and you could come home at weekends sometimes! Letters just aren't the same. You always seem to write in such a rush, too, not even saying what you've been doing half the time.'

'There never seems to be a spare minute for writing proper letters. I go out a lot, there's always something on – like the symphony concerts in the Town Hall. They don't cost much to get in.'

'Symphony – what's that when it's at home?' Cathy asked.

'Oh honestly, Cathy, don't be so ignorant! It's orchestra music, people playing different instruments all together, violins and flutes and things. Beethoven's Fifth, they played.'

'Beethoven's fifth what?'

'Symphony, you idiot! Mum, it's utterly disgraceful what these kids don't know!'

'You always were very musical, Gracie, singing in the church choir and everything,' Mum said. 'It's a great pity we never had the money to have you taught piano.'

'Yes,' Grace said. 'Yes, it is a pity about the piano lessons . . . '

'You'd probably find you had quite a lot in common with Miss Tully, you know. She's fond of music, too. She used to sing at people's weddings when she was younger, all those nice old songs like "Bluebird of Happiness" and "I'll Walk Beside You" . . . '

'Oh Mum, for heaven's sake! You haven't got the faintest . . . '

'Why don't we clear up and have a game of cards like we always used to after tea?' Heather suggested quickly, not quite sure whose feelings she was protecting.

Grace said that she hadn't really played cards for months, felt tired from the train trip, and preferred to go to bed. 'But we'll catch up on all the news in the morning,' she said enthusiastically enough.

In the morning, however, Anthony Robinson called early to drive her up the river to visit the Grantbys. Heather watched them leave, observing that Anthony, despite his ears, was actually quite handsome, and that Grace smiled at him as though discovering immense improvements. Grace herself looked quite stunning, and Heather felt numb with jealousy at her gift of being able to transform the most ordinary materials into things of beauty. Like her plain leather gloves, a pair discarded long ago by Aunt Ivy – Grace had cut them to wrist-length and added cuffs made from knitted string, fastened with small leather buttons. Her paisley scarf was also old, but the colours were beautiful and glowing, and she'd knotted it in a special way so that the fringed ends trailed artistically over the shoulders of her beige jacket. She's like the illustration of a heroine in some magazine story, Heather thought enviously, and quite out of kilter with her own mundane plans for the day, she slumped on the veranda and watched Cathy teeter all around the paddock on the top of the rail fence.

The sobering thought struck her that although she'd done that herself yesterday, madly whirling her arms to balance, such juvenile pastimes should now be discarded. If she wanted to sit in a car next to a personable young man one day and talk knowledgeably about symphony concerts, she'd have to start changing her ways. Yesterday, she thought, with a panicky sensation as though something had been wrenched from her, she'd most likely played her very last game in the paddock with Cathy and Vivienne! But there was no reason to feel melancholy about it, childhood had to come to an end for everyone sooner or later. Grace had made the transition so easily, all she had to do was follow that stylish example, perhaps even catch up and overtake her.

Heather Melling, she thought dreamily, listening to conversations in her head. The belle of Wilgawa . . . The eldest girl had such class, it was only natural her sister should turn out the same. Inseparable, they are, those two lovely charming girls strolling around town arm in arm, more like girlfriends than sisters . . .

Cathy tumbled heavily off the last rail, pretended it had been a calculated victory leap, and came rollicking up to the veranda steps. Heather said distantly, 'You're so rowdy – *must* you always charge about like a drunken sailor?'

'That reminds me, I'm going to make a little jetty thingamyjig down by the river,' Cathy said. 'Want to lend a hand? Maybe we could pinch some of the loose planks out of the shed wall – Dad mightn't notice if we shoved junk across the gap.'

'You leave everything in the shed alone. Dad's going to be in a lousy mood when he gets back, trailing all the way up North and still not landing that fencing contract.'

'Mum reckons he's not coming home straight off.'

'I knew that,' Heather snapped, even though she didn't.

'I don't see how you could have,' Cathy said smugly. 'Seeing it was *me* told to run and fetch Mum because there was a call for her on the brickworks phone. Only fifteen minutes ago, so you *couldn't* have known. I don't know what's up with you lately, Heather, the way you bite people's heads off and never want to do anything any more . . . '

'I certainly don't want to muck around building stupid little jetties that just get washed away! Go away and stop pestering me, go away and play with Vivienne.'

'Don't you want to hear the rest about Dad? He's gone off to look at some cheap land he heard about, and he won't be back till some time next week. Grace'll be pleased. I know someone who most likely wouldn't even be hanging around our place if Dad was home – all Grace's boyfriends have been petrified of Dad! Isobel and me were talking about Anthony Robinson yesterday – want to hear what *she* thinks?'

'Not particularly,' Heather said, examining her outstretched legs critically and deciding to go on a rigorous diet starting from today. Even though Mum was planning to make golden syrup dumplings for tea, she'd just have a pear instead. There were so many things she should do – borrow a book about music from the library, refine her table-manners, never again use vulgar expressions like 'drongo', learn how to tie a scarf in that smart way girls who'd lived in the city seemed to know by instinct . . .

'Grace came home on purpose to get engaged to him, that's what Isobel reckons!' Cathy said. 'And Isobel should know with all those *True Romance* magazines she's got in the carton under her bed. Anthony Robinson hasn't taken any other girl out since Grace left – Isobel said so, and she can always rattle off just who's going out with who in Wilgawa.'

'Rot. Grace only came home because that place where she works has the painters in, she already told us . . . '

'You just wait and see. Isobel says Anthony's the best catch in town, with that furniture store he got when his dad died. *And* property all over the district, too, so if he and Grace get married, he might let us live in one of those houses and not pay rent! Those Robinsons are posh and he wouldn't want his in-laws making him feel embarrassed.'

'Don't be so ridiculous, Cathy, and don't talk like that, either! It sounds awful, like you're making out Grace is chasing him for his money. She doesn't even like him that much, anyhow, he's just someone she used to go to dances and tennis and things with. But there was always a whole lot of them together in a crowd . . . '

'Maybe he'll give us new furniture for free, too,' Cathy said, unsquashed. 'Just think – he might be popping the question right this very minute while they're out on their drive! Grace *Robinson* – doesn't that sound weird?'

'Nick off, you prattling little drongo, you're just as

bad as Isobel spreading gossip around,' Heather said, but was intrigued enough to take a sudden interest in tidying the front garden. To her disappointment, Grace just got out of Anthony Robinson's car when she came back and waved a casual goodbye, not looking at all transformed. Heather knew that a person who'd had a romantic question popped at them surely wouldn't come barging up the front path muttering about the bumpiness of the river road and what a crashing bore Eleanor Grantby was. Feeling cheated, Heather looked bitterly at the huge pile of fallen leaves she'd raked up and the weed-free garden beds, but reminded herself that Grace's visit home wasn't over yet.

Next day, despite Mum's insistence on a round of visits to all the Wilgawa and district relatives, Grace managed to vanish for quite a long time on business of her own.

'Not really on her own,' Cathy gloated, coming back from the shops. 'I spotted her having a peach sundae in the café with you-know-who, and – how about this – she scooped the cherry off the top and popped it into his mouth! I checked up with Isobel on my way home, she reckons that's a romantic thing to do, even though I think it's pretty unhygienic myself . . . '

'Grace doesn't like cherries. She probably just didn't want to waste it.'

'Well, there's that party she's going to tonight. Grace *hates* parties, but you notice she's not making excuses to back out of this one. Anthony and her are most likely going to stand up and make an announcement at it – Isobel said so. Betcha she comes home tonight wearing an engagement ring!'

'That party was arranged ages ago, before anyone even

knew Grace was coming home for a few days. *And* it happens to be for Margaret Edwards' birthday, so it's not very likely they'd use it for announcing their engagement,' Heather jeered, but before going to bed, she secretly snibbed the front door to have an excuse to get up later and let Grace in. Somehow it seemed immensely important that *she* should be the first to receive any romantic confidences, not Cathy or Vivienne. But Grace, coming home much earlier than expected, just marched in full of indignation about being locked out and having to bang on the door.

After lunch next day Mum cut a great pile of sand-wiches for the train trip, even though Grace said she didn't want them. Mum prepared them all the same, looking so downcast that Heather waited until Grace went off to pack her suitcase and then said, 'Grace is being a bit selfish really, though that's nothing new. It's a pity she didn't show more interest in that job with Miss Tully. She *knows* how things are at home right now, this bad patch we're going through. She's the eldest, and she should . . . '

'It's Grace's decision to finish that course, and I won't stand in her way,' Mum said loyally. 'I want all you girls to have something better in life, not have to battle along. And I won't have you sticking your nose in, either, Heather, and making her feel guilty about it – you're not to say one word! We'll manage somehow, we always do. If that land Dad's gone off to look at is half-way decent, he'll get stuck into clearing it and eventually build some kind of house. Depends if we can get the bank loan, of course, depends on a lot of things. But I don't want you spoiling Grace's last afternoon at home by harping on family troubles! You go and help her pack, it will be nice for the two of you to have a bit of a chat . . . '

'It's just . . . you look so sad about her going away again . . . '

'Rubbish,' Mum said fiercely. 'Can't keep you all tied to my apron strings for the rest of your lives, can I? Got to spread your wings . . . '

Heather, unsure of her welcome, went to watch Grace pack her suitcase, but when it was finished, received a flattering surprise. Grace glanced at her watch and whispered, 'Listen, there's *hours* yet before that wretched train leaves. Can you dream up some tactful way to get me out of here? I want to buy poor old Mum a box of chocolates to cheer her up – anyone would think I was off to the North Pole the way she carries on. You can come down to the shops with me if you like, but for heaven's sake don't let on to Vivienne and Cathy! They'll only want to tag along, and I've had about as much as I can stand of their chatter!'

Heather, elated at the thought of Grace wanting her company and hers alone, went back to the kitchen. She suggested, in a voice as smooth as ribbon, a surprise afternoon tea of freshly made raisin scones before Grace left to catch the train. Mum said delightedly, 'What a good idea! How about taking Grace out for a walk while I get it ready? You could take her over to see the new Assembly Hall at the high school for half an hour – perhaps make it one hour, then I'd have time to make a nice cinnamon cake, too.'

Grace, in gratitude, let Heather choose the chocolates when they reached the shops. Heather couldn't remember one other time when they'd walked along Main Street with so much camaraderie. Six months – oh, I'm going to *miss* her! I *need* her here, she thought, feeling oddly devastated. Overcome by the confusion of regarding Grace as anything but a snooty, opinionated older sister whose comings and goings didn't matter in the least, she said quickly, 'Look, you mightn't have noticed – Osborne's have a shoe department now. And they've started widening the little lane so traffic can get through to Haymarket Street . . . '

But Grace had halted in front of the jeweller's shop and was gazing intently at the window display. It couldn't be the shelf of watches that had caught her attention, Heather thought, for she had a watch already, but . . . it could be the display of engagement rings! Perhaps Anthony Robinson really had proposed, just as Cathy said he might! The fact that Grace hadn't said anything about it didn't mean much, she always had been reserved and apt to keep things to herself. Very likely she'd accepted, but had told him he'd have to wait until she'd finished her dressmaking course. That course – even at school she'd never been one for leaving tasks lying about unfinished, everything in her life always so manicured and orderly . . . Heather could recall her sitting up late at night to complete detested school projects, staying home from the beach because she had to study for an exam next day. And even when she'd left school and started work, it had been the same – clothes for the next day carefully ironed and laid out in readiness.

'I'd like a dark red dress one day,' Grace murmured. 'Exactly the same colour as that ring . . . garnet, I think it's called. A lovely colour, just like wine. I'd design it all by myself . . . '

A bride's going-away dress! Heather thought excitedly. Just because she was making Anthony Robinson wait surely wouldn't prevent her dreaming about the actual wedding! She'd probably be making secret plans already, Grace always liked to have things perfectly done, down to the last small detail. Hilary Melling's wedding would be *nothing* compared to it – and most likely Grace had already decided to have just Heather as a bridesmaid! Who would choose to have immature little girls like Cathy and Vivienne follow them, giggling, down the church aisle? *They* certainly hadn't been invited by Grace to go shopping on her last morning at home . . . '

'Diamond rings are really beautiful, too, aren't they?' Heather said meaningfully, basking in the wonderful empathy of strolling along Main Street with Grace, looking in shop windows together as though any age difference had shrunk to a negligible barrier. Such empathy should lead to secrets being shared . . .

'Yes, but everyone always picks diamond engagement rings,' Grace said. 'You can hardly even tell the difference between Margaret Edwards' one and Eleanor Grantby's. I'll be choosing something more unusual when . . . '

Heather held her breath. At any moment now Grace would confide in her, as though they were best friends, perhaps even ask her not to tell another soul, certainly not Cathy or Vivienne just yet . . .

'Goodness, Mr Ulster never seems to change his window display from one year to the next,' Grace said absently. 'I swear that's the same old dusty blue velvet that was there when we had the farm and Mum used to bring us into town once a month on the mail-van. Remember those days?'

'Not really. I would have been too small, and Cathy and Viv only babies then,' Heather said, but a hazy image rippled across her mind, a picture of herself instructed to cling to the side of a pram and not let go, trudging along on fat little legs that wobbled with tiredness. The haziness cleared, and she suddenly remembered with startling vividness the pram being wheeled into a park, a checked blanket spread on the ground, the frantic terror of watching Mum in her straw hat with the flowers walking away, walking through a strange little gate that turned mysteriously around instead of opening. But . . . hadn't there been someone else there, too, someone surely no more than seven or eight, but exuding confidence and self-possession? That someone had said calmly, 'Mum's just gone to ask the shop lady if she can heat up the baby's bottle. She'll come back soon. Don't cry, Heather, people will think you're a sookie if you cry like that. You sit here on the blanket, stay right here on the blanket. I'm going to look at the pretty flowers . . . ' Her own short legs stumbling through grass, tripping on things, her own voice wailing in panic, 'Wait for me, Grace! Oh, wait for me . . . '

'Mum always let us look in Ulster's shop window as a treat, she'd cross the road specially,' Grace said. 'Isn't it funny how you see things as a kid? I always thought this window was like a magic cave, everything so glittery and sparkling – but it's really just a few trays of cheap rings and marcasite watches. Remember during the war when he had a little model of Hitler in the window, trapped inside a set of shark's teeth? That's gone now, he's taken it out, but it's about the only thing that's changed in the whole of Main Street . . . '

'Oh, go on, Grace, there's lots of new things happened since you've been away!'

'Such as?'

'Well . . . there's Osborne's shoe department and the lane being widened. And they might be going ahead with the new bridge over the river,' Heather said, and then, blessed with a dazzling idea, added craftily, 'Let's walk up to the corner and look at the photos in the *Gazette* window.'

The *Gazette* office was next to Robinson's furniture store, and Anthony could very likely be attending to the window display. He'd leave what he was doing, his face lighting up at the unexpected sight of pretty Grace, and come out to the footpath. He'd stand there chatting, Heather thought, only she would hastily remember some little article of shopping she had to do, and leave him alone with Grace. For Grace, she thought with a surge of unhappiness, was going back this afternoon with nothing resolved, no word said, nothing to anchor her here unless . . . 'Come on, let's go and look at the *Gazette* photos,' she urged, but Grace shook her head.

'Those photos are always the same – someone's fat wife wearing a revolting big orchid, or people smirking over potty little awards they've won at the Show. I've got far more interesting things to think about.'

Anthony Robinson really has proposed to her, that's what she means! Heather thought, aching with happiness. Oh, he has! She's only going back to the city to finish that course – and six months isn't all that long when you think about it. It doesn't matter that she didn't take the job with Miss Tully, Mum will get along somehow, she always does. And in the spring Grace will come home to Wilgawa for good, she'll be busy making her trousseau for the wedding . . . Mum's going to be so happy, something nice happening to our family for a change! Grace married to Anthony Robinson and living right here in town, I'll be able to visit her any time I like, she'll teach me things, maybe I'll grow up just as pretty and smart . . .

'Even if you don't want to look at the photos, the *Gazette's* got this . . . this lovely new sunblind over the window. It's really unusual, sort of like a little canopy . . . ' she gabbled, desperately wanting all those things to be confirmed. But Grace had turned aside and was walking away, through the little park towards the riverbank. Heather, tripping over a grass tussock, hurried after her. 'Where are you going?' she called. 'Grace! We've got to get that two o'clock bus back home so you can . . . '

'It's only half-past one,' Grace said. 'And I'm going to have hours and hours of being cooped up on that awful train. Oh, if there's one thing I just can't stand, it's being cooped up! I think I'll go for a nice long run now while I've got the chance . . . '

'Hang on a minute, I can't keep up!' Heather complained, stumbling over Grace's shoes, which had been kicked off and left at the top of the steps leading down to the river. Heather bent to retrieve them with faint disapproval, for people of Grace's age didn't run about without shoes in Wilgawa, it just wasn't done . . . Specially not if they were going to be Mrs Anthony Robinson and live in that lovely big house over on the east bank.

'Here – catch!' Grace cried, snatching off her paisley scarf and tossing it back over her shoulder.

'Your hair's come down all over the place!' Heather said.

'You sound just like Aunty Ivy, and who cares, any-how? Oh, those ghastly visits to Aunt Ivy and all the others! This is the most boring little place in the whole world, same old shops and same old people and conversations! So *bored* . . . having to put up with that dreary Anthony Robinson because I couldn't be nasty to him when his father's just died. But now it's nearly over and I'll be going back home to the beautiful, beautiful city!'

Back . . . home.

Grace ran along the riverbank with her long hair adrift. She didn't stop to pin it up, but tilted her face joyously to the sky and spread her arms like wings. A cold wind blew over the water, scattering leaves from the poplar trees, showering her with golden coins.

Heather stood quite still, watching, feeling so desolate she could hardly bear it. She became aware that the sun had disappeared behind a mass of banked clouds, that the season was drawing to a close and winter coming, that the river suddenly looked bleak. There was a sensation of weight upon her shoulders, of a burden that was perhaps beyond her capabilities.

I've become the eldest in the family now, I'm not ready for it, she thought, panicking, and opened her mouth to call out, 'Wait for me! Oh, Grace, wait for me, I want to come with you . . . ' But Grace had disappeared around the curve where the willows grew, and Heather made no move to follow, not sure if she'd ever catch up.